THE LOCHVIEW MYSTERIES

The Lady of the Loch

Ryan Vernel

1

It was moving day.

"Tyler, are you ready yet?" Mum called, her voice drifting in through my open bedroom window. Outside I could hear the car's engine growling gently, but I still needed a moment more. Looking down from my room I could see her standing, hands on hips, in the front garden.

"Nearly there," I shouted back. "I'm just grabbing my bag."

With a sigh, I turned back to my empty room. The last few weeks since school broke up had gone by in a whirlwind. I spent my holidays running around the town with my friends. We'd played football in the streets, taken our bikes down to the river, even snuck into the old burnt-out house down by the train tracks.

It had been a summer to remember, but now I was leaving it all behind.

It felt strange.

Last night I fell asleep in Oxford and tomorrow I'll be waking up in Scotland.

New friends, new school, a whole new life.

I zipped up my backpack and threw it over my shoulder. Inside it was loaded with comics and puzzles, snacks and games, anything to help fight the boredom of what my sister had spent the week describing as the world's longest car journey.

I took one final look at my room, not that it felt like it was mine anymore. There was no bed, no TV, no posters on the wall. All the things that made it feel like home.

"Come on mate, we need to get on the road. We've got a long drive ahead of us."

It was my dad, he leant against the door frame, smiling softly at me.

"Yeah, I'm just coming now," I replied.

"A lot of memories in this room," he said, looking around.

I didn't really know how to respond. This little blue box had been my room all my life. That was twelve years of video games and bedtime stories, of water fights and movie nights. I remember one time my dad sat down to read me and my sister a story, only for Emily to make him laugh so hard his drink came out his nose. In fact, I was sure if I looked hard enough, I could probably find the stain on the carpet.

I loved my room.

Not that my parents cared. Mum and Dad had decided they wanted to make a change, they called it a new adventure, so now we were all moving to some tiny town in Scotland called Lochview.

Mum had found a small café for sale on the high street there. She spent weeks discussing it with Dad, until one night they sat me and Emily down at the table and told us they had bought it.

"Are you going to miss this place?"

"A little." I shrugged. "Not that it really matters what I think."

"Of course it matters what you think." He placed his hand on my shoulder. "Tyler, this move is a really big opportunity for all of us, not just your mum and I. You're thirteen next year, that's a big deal, so this is the perfect time to start looking forward. We've got a chance here to really build a future, all I ask is that you trust me and give it a chance. Is that fair?"

I considered for a moment.

"Yeah, that's fair." I nodded.

"Thank you." He stood up straight and looked over my shoulder into the room. "You know, I think there is still one last thing we need to do before we leave."

He stepped past me.

Dad had a playful look in his eye and the kind of smile that told me whatever he was about to do was not Mum-approved. He moved to the corner of the room, and crouching down, he carefully pulled back the carpet, revealing the floorboards underneath. Reaching into his pocket he slid out a small penknife.

I kept watching as he used it to slice into the boards. Cut after cut, very precise and very exact.

After a couple of moments, he was done and stood up to admire his handiwork.

He waved me over. Looking down, I saw three words carved into the wood below.

TYLER WAS HERE!

With his arm around my shoulders, he squeezed me tight.

"Now no one will ever forget that this was your room."

I had no words, so I simply looked up at him and smiled.

"Come on, grab your bag and let's head downstairs," he said, pushing the carpet back into place. "We don't want your mum coming up here and seeing this, I'd be in big trouble then."

I chuckled as I walked out of my room for the very last time. With one final glance back over my shoulder, I went downstairs.

"Are we ready to go?" Mum asked as Dad stopped to lock the front door.

"Ready," I confirmed.

"OK, are you jumping in the car with me and your sister or the van with your dad?"

It was a good question, I hadn't really thought about it.

"I would certainly appreciate the company," Dad said, as I looked awkwardly between them. "What do you say? Fancy a road trip with your old man?"

"Yeah, sure," I replied.

"Perfect, well let's get this show on the road." Mum turned towards the car parked in the road, Emily was perched against it with her head in her phone. "Come on Em, get your butt in the car, we're going on a girl's trip."

I watched in embarrassment as Mum did what could only be described as a kind of excited dance over to the car.

"We shall see you boys in Scotland!" she shouted, with a cheer and a wave as she climbed into the driver's seat.

"Let's just pretend that didn't happen," Dad said, under his breath.

"Agreed." I followed him to the van and got in.

As I placed my backpack at my feet, Dad reached into the glovebox and pulled out a plastic bag.

"Before we head off, I've got something for you," he said. "I thought it might help you get a little more excited about Lochview."

I reached inside and pulled out a book.

Haunted Scotland.

I could feel a smile spread across my face. I'd always loved a good ghost story. We used to have a tradition where every Halloween Emily and I would build pillow forts and tell each other tales of ghosts and ghouls. We'd even hold a torch under our chin for that real creep factor.

Not that she would do it anymore, she was too old for that.

"Here, there's something I want you to see." Dad opened the book and handed it back to me.

As he placed it in my hands the chapter title immediately caught my eye.

The Lady of the Loch.

2

I barely even noticed the van start moving.

From the moment the book was in my hands I was hooked.

A black-and-white picture of a large manor house stood boldly at the top of the page. It looked like something out of a horror movie with stone walls and heavy wooden doors, framed on either side by rows upon rows of large windows. All along the roof stood a line of battlements, like the medieval castles I'd seen on school trips.

If ever a house could look haunted, this one definitely ticked all the boxes.

Lochview Manor stands on the shores of Loch Dowell, its shadow casting far across the murky waters. Built in 1356 by Lord Dowell, it has been the home to nobility for many centuries, housing not just Lords and Ladies, but also the secrets that they keep. Stories of restless spirits are rife within its hallowed halls, but none so striking, or so deadly, as The Lady of the Loch.

I felt goosebumps run up my arm. With each word my excitement grew. When Mum and Dad first told me about moving to Lochview I couldn't think of anything worse. A small town in the middle of nowhere, surrounded by nothing but hills and trees and nature, was the definition of boring. Yet, they never mentioned this, the real-life haunted manor sitting right on the edge of town.

A manor with not just any ghost, but a *deadly* ghost.

I was starting to think this wouldn't be so boring after all.

Recorded sightings of the Lady are few and far between. Of those that did put their experiences into writing, some tell of a young woman in a flowing white dress, wandering lost and alone through the halls of the manor, whilst others describe her watching them across the dark waters of the loch. Either way, according to legend, her presence in Lochview comes at a terrible price.

Local folklore suggests that the Lady of the Loch was wronged in her previous life, perhaps the victim of a dramatic betrayal, or a soul taken in a grisly murder. Whatever the method of her demise, it is her revenge from beyond the grave for which she will be remembered. It is well known in the town of

Lochview that no child should dare to misbehave, lest they wake The Lady from her watery grave.

This story has run deep within the fabric of life in Lochview for hundreds of years, with the Lady of the Loch being blamed for the disappearance of many children in the area. Yet, despite plenty of theories, many questions still remain; who is this restless spirit, where did she come from, and what does she want with the children of Lochview?

I looked over at my dad. His eyes focused forward on the road ahead.

"Dad, do you believe in ghosts?" I asked.

"I don't know," he said. "I guess I haven't really thought about it."

I turned and looked out the window.

I believed in ghosts.

I knew that much at least. I'm not sure what it was, but something in my gut told me they had to be real. There had to be something out there, something lurking in the shadows, why else would we be afraid of the dark?

"Maybe Lochview will have the answer," Dad said, raising an eyebrow.

Maybe he was right.

My stomach was swimming with a mixture of nerves and excitement. The thought of being face-to-face with an actual ghost was equal parts brilliant and terrifying.

9

As far as I could tell there was just one thing I had to do to make it happen.

I had to solve the mystery of the Lady of the Loch.

3

Welcome to Lochview.

Dad woke me with a nudge and pointed to the sign standing behind a neatly kept flower bed.

It was nearly sunset as we drove into the centre of town. Everywhere I looked along the high street were shops selling scarves and jackets, or jewellery and little glass figures.

Where were the normal shops?

I wasn't interested in any of that rubbish.

"Do you want to see something cool?" Dad asked.

"Yeah, go for it," I replied, not that there was much to beat so far.

Dad turned down a side street and brought the van to a stop.

"Welcome to the all-new Buckland Café," he announced.

"Where is it?" I looked up and down the road but didn't see anything that resembled a café.

"Right there." Dad jumped out of the van and stood proudly in front of a pair of boarded-up windows.

I stepped out and joined him.

I couldn't understand what was so exciting. The café was nestled, small and abandoned, amongst a row of shops. If it wasn't for the large red sold sign sticking out above the door you might not have even noticed it was there.

"It might not look like much now," Dad admitted. "But your mum and I have got big plans for this place. With a little hard work and elbow grease, we'll be the talk of the town."

I was going to have to take his word for it. All I could see were broken windows and chipped paint. The place looked like a dump.

Not that I could tell my dad that.

"Yeah, it looks cool," I said, forcing a smile.

Dad put his arm around my shoulders and smiled back.

"Right, come on," he said. "We best get going. Your mum will be wondering where we are."

Jumping in the van, we headed back to the main road.

There was only one place left to see in Lochview, and that was our new house.

I didn't actually know too much about it. Mum was going to show me and my sister pictures, but Dad said to leave it as a surprise. All she told us was it's a cottage on the edge of the town and it looks out over the loch.

Knowing my luck it would be like something out of a fairy tale. White painted walls, with big wooden beams and a thatched roof. All pretty, and lovely, and boring. Though I guess, if it meant I got a bigger room with space on the wall for a widescreen TV, then it wouldn't be all bad.

According to the satnav, we were only a couple of minutes away.

Outside, the shops and houses had come to an end and had been replaced by countryside. Though I only caught little glimpses past the high hedgerows that ran along either side of the road.

"You have arrived at your destination."

I looked around in confusion. The satnav had to be wrong, there was nothing here.

The van slowed as two large iron gates appeared in the hedge to our right. Dad turned between them, leading us onto a small dark road.

"What going on?" I asked.

"We're here," Dad replied, a smile spreading across his face. "Welcome to your new home."

As we continued along the road a huge manor house came into view. The stone walls, the large wooden doors, the battlements along the roof, I recognised it instantly.

Lochview Manor.

"We're living here?"

"Not quite." Dad laughed. "There's an old gamekeeper cottage around the back. That's where we'll be living, but I'm sure if you ask nicely they'll let you have a look around."

I couldn't believe my eyes.

As we carried on down the road the house just kept getting bigger and bigger, it seemed to keep stretching on forever. I had to lean forward in my seat just to look up at the roof.

Just before the manor, the road forked, Dad turned and drove us down to our cottage.

I sat back brimming with excitement.

This was insane.

I wasn't just living *near* a haunted manor house.

I was living next door.

"Where have you been?" Mum called at us as we pulled up outside the cottage.

"Sorry, we took a slight detour," Dad replied, leaning out the window. "Thought we'd take in a few of the sights."

Climbing out of the van I recoiled at the sight of our new home.

It looked like it was falling down.

The house itself was an old stone cottage. A crooked wooden fence caged an overgrown garden, full of long grass, weeds, and who knows what else. The branches of a huge tree reached threateningly towards the roof, poised as if ready to knock the house down at the slightest hint of a breeze. The windows were dark and dreary, the paint was peeling off the front door, and the chimney looked ready to jump.

Mum was right about one thing though, it stood right on the edge of the loch. In fact, had it been any closer I'd have been sharing my room with a fish.

"We're living *here*?" I asked, turning to Dad.

"Give it a chance," he replied. "Just trust me."

He seemed to be saying that a lot lately.

Mum dropped a suitcase at my feet.

"Come on, let's get inside," she said, grabbing another bag. "No point standing out here."

I grabbed the case and followed her to the door.

Stepping inside I walked into a large kitchen, just as old and forgotten as the outside of the house. Emily sat with her feet up on a big wooden dining table in the middle of the room.

"Decided to show up then?" she said, looking up from her phone.

"Em, get your feet off the table and give us a hand with these bags," Mum scolded.

Emily swung her legs down with a huff, I turned away from her and smirked.

"Did you see the big house?" Em continued, walking towards me. "Looks pretty old, I'd be careful if I was you, it's probably haunted."

Out of the corner of my eye, I saw Dad smile at me. Little did my sister know just how right she might be.

"Right then, we've all had a pretty long day so I think we can let the boxes wait until tomorrow," he said, leaning against the kitchen counter. "How about you two head upstairs and choose your rooms?"

A sudden tension filled the air.

Me and Emily exchanged looks, both primed and ready to run, waiting for the other to flinch. My sister was quick, there was no denying it, but I was quicker. Her head twitched and I was off. I burst out of the kitchen and into the living room, almost knocking over a lamp on the way. I heard the faint sound of Mum telling us not to run but it was too late.

Emily tried to grab me as I reached the bottom of the stairs, but I shrugged myself free from her grip. I clambered upwards towards the landing, a wide smile on my face.

I was winning.

As I reached the top of the stairs, I was confronted with four doors. I felt the pressure rise as I suddenly realised I had to make a decision, and fast. Emily wasn't going to let me choose twice.

The door in front of me stood open. Through it I could see a large double room. It was clearly Mum and Dad's so there was no point choosing that.

Three doors left.

I felt my sister's hands on my back, trying to barge past. I had to make a choice.

Door two!

Something in my gut told me it was the one. There was no time for doubt, so I went for it, reaching out my hand I felt the metal handle at my fingertips.

"Bagsy this one," I called out triumphantly, panting hard.

I pulled open the door to reveal my prize. The thrill of victory was pumping through every inch of my body and the smile on my face couldn't hide my smugness.

My sister came and stood beside me, looking over my shoulder as the door creaked open.

The bathroom.

"Well, the bath certainly looks comfortable," she mocked. "I, however, will probably go for one of the bedrooms. I'm just weird like that."

Emily strolled casually to the next door to reveal a second double room.

"If you need me, I'll just be in here." She laughed, closing the door behind her.

I went back to the first door with my head hung low. As I pushed it open, I was instantly hit by the smell of dust and damp. I dropped my bag on the bare wooden floor and flopped on my bed with a thud.

I looked around with a sigh, the room was even smaller than the one I'd had back in Oxford. It was just empty white walls and a solitary window looking out over the darkness of the loch. About as warm and inviting as a prison cell.

As I lay there listening to the wind whistling outside, I had only one thought on my mind.

I hate Lochview.

5

I was sitting in my pyjamas, staring at my suitcase from the corner of my bed. For a moment I considered unpacking, but quickly came to the decision that it was a job for tomorrow. It was getting late, and I wasn't in the mood to sort through everything.

Through the floor beneath me, I could hear my parents talking in the kitchen.

"How was he on the drive up?" I heard Mum ask, her voice sounded worried.

"He was alright," Dad said. "I think he liked the book. He asked me if I believe in ghosts."

"And what did you say?"

"I told him the truth," Dad replied. "He shouldn't be worrying about ghosts, not with that monster under his bed."

Dad started laughing whilst Mum told him off.

As their conversation gradually drifted onto the Café, I started getting bored. I lay back on my bed and

19

stared at the ceiling, mapping all the stains and cracks in the paint.

I felt alone.

I felt like I was trapped in this prison cell of a room, miles away from anything, with nothing but my suitcase for company, and it sucked. It sucked big time.

With a sigh, I rolled over and turned off my lamp.

It was time for sleep.

Hopefully, the morning would bring something new, but for now, the cold itchy bed sheets Mum had borrowed from the manor were just adding to my list of problems.

The hours rolled by as I stared at the ceiling waiting for sleep to arrive. I lay there as the rest of my family began to wind down. I heard my sister in the bathroom brushing her teeth, my parents sneaking quietly to bed trying not to wake us. I was still wide awake as my dad drifted off, signalled by his loud snoring, sort of like a pig with a cold. Not to be outdone by Mum, who moments later joined in.

I picked my phone up off the bedside table.

1:00am.

I groaned, burying my head in the pillow. Try as I might, sleep just would not come. I climbed out of bed and headed to the door, maybe a drink would help me nod off.

As I walked into the kitchen I fumbled around the wall for the light switch. The tiled floor was cold against my bare feet.

Click.

The light blinked a couple of times before filling the room. I covered my eyes, they took a moment to adjust from the darkness of the rest of the house. I looked through the cupboards for a glass, but other than a thick layer of dust they were all empty.

I turned to a large box sitting on the kitchen table.

Yes!

I reached in and found a bunch of glasses wrapped in bubble wrap. I peeled it off and went to the sink.

Needless to say, it was gross.

The cracked orange tiles on the wall were speckled with black, the surface was sticky and stained, even the tap itself had a huge cobweb hanging off it.

Suddenly I wasn't feeling very thirsty anymore.

"Tyler."

I froze. Glancing over my shoulder, I looked for the source of the voice. It was nothing more than a soft whisper but still there was no one with me.

I put my glass in the sink and walked back to the living room.

"Tyler."

There it was again. I looked towards the door. Maybe it was coming from outside?

"Hello? Is anyone there?" I asked, keeping my voice low. I didn't want to wake anyone else in the house.

Nothing. I reached out for the handle. I felt it cold in my hand.

"Tyler, what are you doing up?"

My mum stood in the doorway to the living room.

"I was just getting a drink," I replied. Trying to hide the fact she had just scared the life out of me.

"Well grab one and get back to bed, we're getting up early in the morning," she rubbed her eyes and headed off into the darkness.

With one last glance at the door, I went back to bed.

I certainly didn't want to be in the kitchen any longer than I had to.

6

My first full day in Lochview was not off to a good start.

I sat at the kitchen table tired and grumpy, munching on a piece of toast. It turned out the curtains in my room weren't big enough to cover the windows. So, when the sun rose this morning, so did I.

Mum on the other hand seemed to be in a very good mood, as she danced around the kitchen, singing along to the radio, much to the dismay of me and my sister.

"Good morning, everyone," Dad announced cheerfully, coming through from the living room.

"Is it?" Emily replied, staring, horrified, at Mum.

"Hey, what are you trying to say?" He grabbed a piece of toast and took a bite. "Your mum is a wonderful dancer, if anything the both of you should watch closely, you might learn a thing or two."

"Oh, stop it." Mum giggled playfully.

Dad put his arms around her and leant in for a kiss. Me and Emily shared a look of disgust.

Taking a seat at the end of the table, Dad proceeded to lay out his plan for the day. It was fairly simple.

Unload boxes.

Unpack boxes.

Repeat until the van is empty.

I sat back in my chair with a groan, just the thought of the day ahead was already exhausting. Over my sister's shoulder, I looked through the window at the sun shining outside. Had I been back in Oxford, I'd have been down by the river or chilling with my friends by the shops. Instead, I was going to be in this stupid house, in stupid Lochview, unpacking stupid boxes.

I'd barely even swallowed the last bite of my breakfast before Dad started marching us out to the van.

The day dragged, no matter how much we removed from the van there always seemed to be more. We carried box after box, bag after bag, and I was beginning to worry it wouldn't all fit in the house.

As the hours passed, the shadow of the manor house crept slowly towards us. I looked up at its large windows and wondered what secrets it had hidden inside.

Slam!

Dad closed the shutter on the van.

"Done!" He placed his hands on his hips. "Well done everyone, that was a lot of stuff."

"Does that mean I can go now?" Emily already had her phone in her hand. "I promised Georgia I'd call her tonight."

"Yes, go," he replied. Though his words were wasted, she was already gone. "What about you, Tyler, what are you going to do?"

I looked up at the manor and then back to my dad.

"I might go for a walk." I shrugged. "Maybe have an explore around the loch."

Dad looked at me suspiciously.

But in my defence, it was at least half true.

I was desperate to explore, but it wasn't at the loch.

I waited until Mum and Dad were out of view and turned back up the road toward the manor. With each step I took, it grew larger and larger, its grey stone bricks towering high above me.

As I came round to the front, I peered in through one of the windows, pressing my face up against the glass. Inside was quite possibly the world's biggest dining table, it must have had about thirty seats around it. Our one in the cottage looked tiny by comparison. Hung above it was a huge chandelier. I'd never seen anything like it, glittering like thousands and thousands of diamonds.

Moving along, I glanced into the next room. Bookcases stretched floor to ceiling, around a large stone fireplace. On the wall above hung a blue shield with a white lion painted on it, and tucked behind it were two crossed swords.

It was the coolest thing ever.

Looking through the windows was like looking back in time. As I kept moving along, I saw more and more pieces of history. Suits of armour, deer antlers, portraits of old Lords standing proud in their tartan colours.

The house was full of trinkets and treasures. With each room I looked in I found the most amazing things I could ever imagine, but there were no signs of anyone actually living there.

I came to the heavy wooden front doors. For a moment I hesitated, feeling a chill on my neck like someone was watching me.

I told myself I was being silly. If there was anyone here, I'd have seen them by now. At the very least there would have been a light on.

I reached out and grabbed the large black iron handle.

Click.

It was open.

With one last glance over my shoulder, I stepped inside.

It was like walking into a palace.

My footsteps echoed on the black and white tiles beneath my feet. A grand staircase climbed along the wooden panels on the wall. At the bottom stood a round table.

My eyes were drawn to a large wooden sculpture of a bird, it stood proudly in the centre of the table. Moving closer I admired its hooked beak and sharp talons, running my fingers along the edges. I think it was some kind of eagle or falcon, it reminded me of the birds of prey I saw last year on a school trip.

"It's a beauty, isn't it?"

I nearly jumped out of my skin. Behind me stood a small round man dressed in a dark green tweed waistcoat and trousers, a red tartan tie and matching red tartan glasses.

His slick brown hair and bushy moustache made him look a little like a walrus.

"It's a Peregrine Falcon, a symbol of great insight and intuition," he continued, pushing his glasses up his nose. He was very well-spoken, yet undeniably Scottish. "Though in Celtic folklore it can be seen as an omen of imminent danger. They believe that Peregrines are messengers from the other side."

"The other side?" I repeated.

"Messages from the dead, young sir." He laughed. "That is a tale for another day, however. I believe now is the time for introductions. My name is Archibald Macleod, Or Archie to my friends. I am the tour guide extraordinaire and font of all knowledge when it comes to the Lochview Manor House. And you must be young master Tyler Buckland?"

"Yeah, how did you know that?" I asked, taken aback.

"It's my business to know," he responded mysteriously. "Plus, I had a wee chat with your mother last night when she came to collect the keys for the cottage."

He chuckled warmly for a moment and then stopped.

"Now, as much as I would love to give you a tour of the old place, I am unfortunately locking up for the night." He fumbled in his pockets and pulled out a set of keys. "I do, however, have a ghost tour tomorrow at two, so you are more than welcome to come back then. But be warned, it is not for the faint of heart."

"Yeah sure, that sounds great, thank you." I stepped backwards, out into the cool evening air.

"Perfect! Though before you go, Tyler. I have just one question," He paused, looking over the rim of his glasses. "What brought you into Lochview Manor this evening? Is it the house that intrigues you, or the secrets that she keeps?"

"I was just curious I guess," I replied, a little taken aback.

"Well now, that is a very good answer indeed." He smiled. "After all, curious is a very wonderful thing to be."

7

Archie was strange.

That's what I decided as I made my way back home. I'd never known anyone like him. His strange little looks, the weird way he spoke, those crazy tartan glasses. He was like a cartoon character come to life.

I smiled to myself. Something about the thought of him shuffling around that big empty house really tickled me.

I looked back up at the manor, excited to think what tomorrow might bring. Maybe Archie could help shed a little light on the mystery of the Lady of the Loch.

For a moment I imagined her, white dress flowing, staring down at me from the battlements.

Standing in the shadow of the house, I made myself a promise.

I'm going to find the Lady of the Loch. I'm going to find her and I'm going to discover who she really is.

A cool breeze sent a shiver down my spine. I needed to get home, it was getting late.

Turning away from the manor I continued down the road. In the distance, I could see the lights on in the cottage.

Snap!

I stopped, looking around for the source of the noise. There was nothing.

A row of large trees lined either side of the road, but other than that there was nowhere to hide.

"Hello?" I called out.

Silence.

I started to feel uneasy, like someone was watching me.

I carried on walking, this time a little faster than before. Then I heard it again.

Snap!

I spun around quickly, but still, there was no one there.

"Very funny, you can come out now," I shouted.

Still silence.

I looked over my shoulder, it was still a fairly long way to the cottage, though I could probably run it if I had to. As my stomach churned nervously, it was starting to look like the safest option.

Snap!

My body tensed, ready to run. There was a soft rustle of leaves as my secret stalker stepped out from behind a tree.

It was a baby deer.

It stepped out into the road, its little legs wobbling beneath it. It was so cool, I'd never seen one this close before.

"Oh, hey there little guy," I said softly.

Cautiously I moved forward, trying not to spook it. As I did it froze, staring at me wide-eyed.

"It's OK, I'm not going to hurt you." I reached my hand out slowly.

It glanced back towards the house, then back to me, and then in a flash, it was gone. Skipping away from me at lightning speed.

I watched in amazement as it zig-zagged its way across the grass.

As it disappeared into the night, something caught my eye. Though most of the manor lay in darkness, there was now a light on, that hadn't been before. It was far away, and I couldn't be sure, but I think I saw a woman watching me.

"Boo!"

I let out a scream as my sister burst into laughter behind me.

"Why would you do that?" I asked, breathing hard.

"Because it's hilarious," Emily replied, with an evil smile. "Where have you been?"

"None of your business." I pushed past her in the direction of home.

"Dad said you were probably out hunting ghosts," she teased. "But I told him that couldn't be right, you'd be too scared."

I could hear her laughing as I walked away, but I wasn't going to let her get to me.

I stole one last secret glance back towards the manor as I reached home. But there was nothing to see. The light was gone.

8

I was late.

I'd spent the morning unpacking my room. Finding homes for all my books, games and DVDs, filling my wardrobe and drawers with all my clothes. I didn't want to, but it was the only way Mum was going to let me go on the ghost tour.

As I threw the last of my jumpers into a drawer I glanced down at my watch.

01:58pm.

I had two minutes. I raced around the house grabbing anything I could possibly need and throwing it in a bag. I had a notepad, I had my pencil case, but I couldn't find the book my dad had given me.

I looked around my neat and tidy room but at first glance, it was nowhere to be seen. There was only one option, but I knew Mum was going to kill me.

I started pulling out drawers and started making piles of everything I had just put away on my bedroom floor. Finally, turning my room upside down, I found it in a drawer under my bed.

Closing the door on the mess I had made I ran downstairs and threw on my shoes.

"Is everything unpacked?" Mum asked as I headed for the door.

"Yep, all done," I replied. Technically it wasn't a lie, everything was unpacked. She should've asked if I had put it all away. "I'll see you later."

I escaped before she had the chance to ask any more questions, and with my backpack slung over my shoulder ran up the road to the manor.

I opened the door to find a large group of tourists gathered by the entrance. I squeezed through, past their cameras and bags, and found myself a place near the front. Looking up I saw the familiar face of Archie taking his position halfway up the stairs.

It looked like I was just in time. The group fell silent as he cleared his throat.

"Ladies and Gentlemen, esteemed guests one and all," he announced. "It is my privilege to welcome each and every one of you to Lochview Manor. This house is steeped in over seven hundred years of history and has been home to nobility throughout the ages. Believe me, if these walls could talk, they would have a story or two to tell, but since they cannot, it falls on me to share the secrets that they keep."

The group looked at each other excitedly. Off to the side, I spotted a boy, about my age, with messy blonde hair, thin round glasses and a backpack that was almost bigger than him. In his hand he held a book that I recognised in an instant.

Haunted Scotland.

Maybe I wasn't the only one interested in the mystery of the Lady of the Loch.

"If you would all like to follow me upstairs, let us start with the master bedroom, a sanctuary for the many Earls of Lochview over the centuries. Though in the case of Lord William Dowell III Ninth Earl of Lochview, it was to be his final resting place." Archie turned dramatically, stopping the group in their tracks. "Some even say that in the dead of night you can hear his spirit calling out for the wife he lost, but the lady never comes."

As the group climbed the stairs, I moved across to the boy on the other side.

"That's a cool book," I said. "I've got the same one in my bag."

"Oh really?" he replied, looking at me oddly.

"My dad got it for me. It was a moving present. I'm Tyler," I said, holding my hand out to him.

"Jackson." He looked down at my hand and shook it gently. "I think we're meant to follow the group."

"Yeah, sure." I followed him up the staircase. There was something a little strange about Jackson, but he seemed nice enough. "Do you mind if I tag along with you? I'm here on my own."

He looked at me for a moment, considering his answer.

"I guess that's OK." He gave a nod and then scurried up the last of the stairs.

We caught up with the group just as Archie took his place by a large four-poster bed. A huge window looking out over the loch took up almost an entire wall, whilst the rest were covered in large wooden panels.

I found a spot with Jackson next to a grand-looking dressing table.

"It was here that Lord William Dowell III drew his final breath. As the end was near, he called out for his wife the Honourable Lady Elizabeth Dowell. Little did he know that she was perhaps not as honourable as she seemed." Archie paused. "Though no evidence was ever found, it was widely believed that his wife had poisoned him, claiming Lochview Manor and its surrounding lands for herself."

"What happened to her?" I turned to see Jackson with his hand raised in the air. "I know that she got married again and had two daughters, but then they just seem to vanish. From what I've read it sounds like the house stood empty for almost a hundred years."

"A very good question young man. It sounds like someone has been doing their research," Archie replied with a smile. "The honest answer is no one knows. There are documents stating that future generations of her family did claim the house, but none seemed to stay for very long. Perhaps the ghost of Lord William drove them away."

Jackson looked away and muttered under his breath. "Or maybe it was something else."

Archie led the group out into the hallway and on to the next room. As everyone filed out, I turned to Jackson.

"You seem to know a lot about this place."

"A little I guess." He shrugged.

"Maybe you could help me?" I asked. "I'm looking for information about the Lady of the Loch."

Something changed in Jackson, there was a hint of excitement in his eyes.

"What do you want to know?"

9

When the tour was finished, I grabbed Jackson and headed for the door.

We had so much to discuss. But not here, not with all these people around.

"Well then boys, what did we think of the tour?" Archie emerged from the crowd, catching us before we could escape.

"It was great, thank you," I replied, smiling politely.

"And educational I hope." He glanced down at the book under Jackson's arm. "Though perhaps I could stand to learn a few things from the two of you. I see you are fans of the paranormal."

"We're looking into the Lady of the Loch," Jackson said confidently. "We're going to uncover her true identity."

"Oh are you? You'll have to let me know what you find, I could add it to the tour." He laughed. "Though a word to the wise, boys. Some secrets aren't meant to be discovered, sometimes the things that go bump in the night don't like it when you bump back."

With a playful wink, Archie wandered back into the group of tourists. Answering questions and taking photos, laughing and joking as he went.

"Come on, let's get out of here," I said, nudging Jackson. "You can come back to mine if you want, my parents won't mind."

"No," he replied, a little abruptly. "If we're going to do this properly then we need somewhere secret. Somewhere away from other people."

"OK, what do you have in mind?" I asked.

"Don't worry, I know somewhere." He pushed past me to the door. "Follow me."

So that's what I did.

I struggled to keep up as Jackson marched down the road towards my house. As home came into view he turned sharply onto a dirt path heading for a thick wood on the edge of the loch.

"Where are we going?" I called after him, as I ducked and weaved through heavy tree branches.

"It's not far," he shouted back, pushing further into the forest.

The deeper we went the darker it got. Looking over my shoulder I couldn't even see the road anymore. The ground was thick with twigs and dead leaves, crunching and snapping as my feet sank into the mud.

"Here we are," Jackson announced.

I stepped out of the trees and into the bright sunlight. I held my hand over my eyes, waiting for them to adjust.

I was standing on a small section of the shore, hidden away from the rest of the world. It was like our own little private beach, just with pebbles and rocks instead of sand.

Jackson sat down on a fallen tree, its branches lay twisted and knotted, reaching out into the waters of the loch.

"This place is awesome," I said, taking it all in.

"I like to come here sometimes to be alone." He reached down into his bag. "Take a seat."

I perched myself on a tree stump, watching as Jackson rummaged deeper and deeper inside his backpack. For a moment I thought he might fall in.

"Here it is," he said triumphantly.

He pulled out a small green leather notepad. A small piece of card on the front bore his name in big capital letters.

JACKSON WEIR.

"What is it?" I asked.

"This is everything I know so far about the Lady of the Loch." He held it out towards me.

I reached out and opened it. Inside was page after page, full of notes. There were lists of victims, timelines of disappearances, even detailed accounts from those that had seen her.

"This is insane," I muttered under my breath.

"It is not *insane*," Jackson corrected. "It is *thorough*. I've read through every book, I've looked through every website, that is everything there is to know about the Lady of the Loch. Well, almost everything. There's still one piece missing. Her name."

"This must have taken you ages." With every page I turned I found more and more notes. "How did you find the time?"

"I don't have many friends," he replied sheepishly, pushing his glasses up his nose.

I closed the book with a slam.

"OK," I said. "Where do we start?"

He looked up at me with a smile.

"We need to go back to the beginning. Go through the stories and find a connection. There is one thing I can't understand, and that is *why*. Why take children? Why in Lochview? I think the answer lies in the manor."

Snap!

Jackson snatched the book from my hand, holding it close as we both looked to the treeline.

Everything went silent, except for the gentle lapping of the waves against the shore.

"Who's there?" I called out. Watching closely for any sign of movement.

For a moment there was nothing, then slowly a girl stepped forward from the shadows.

She was the most Scottish-looking person I'd ever seen in my life, her long red hair hung wild over her shoulders, and her green eyes were piercing against her pale skin.

"I'll be honest," she said, holding her hands up in surrender. "I think your pal here is onto something."

"How much did you hear?" I questioned.

"Enough to know you're investigating the Lady of the Loch," she replied. "And I want in."

10

Her name was Shona.

And honestly, she was kind of awesome.

Jackson was clearly nervous about sharing his precious notes with anyone else, I think even sharing them with me was a big deal to him, but slowly he started to open up. He listened intently as she told us about a friend of hers who had actually seen the Lady herself.

"She's eight feet tall, with rotting skin and fangs that could tear you into pieces," Shona said, her eyes almost as wide as her smile.

Jackson looked puzzled.

"I'm not sure that is quite right," he said, causing me and Shona to burst out laughing.

The afternoon rolled by as we sat reading through Jackson's notebook. We suggested theory after theory, from the boring and sensible to the downright insane, yet we always came to the same conclusion. It just didn't fit.

"OK, hear me out," Shona said. "What if the Lady of Loch isn't a lady?"

"What?" I asked confused.

"Well, what if it's actually some guy with long hair, wearing a kilt and people just think it's a woman?" She smiled. "Maybe we've found the ghost of William Wallace and he's recruiting children to join his army against the English? Just saying, Tyler, you might want to watch out."

"People have seen her, Shona. We know she's a woman," Jackson said, unimpressed.

"But has anyone seen her in the daytime?" she continued. "Sometimes it can be hard to tell in the dark."

"If this is just a joke to you then maybe you shouldn't be here at all." Jackson's face went bright red. I looked awkwardly between him and Shona, waiting for someone to say something.

"Alright, chill out, I was just having a laugh," Shona said, crossing her arms.

"Maybe we should stop for the day?" I suggested, trying to calm things down.

Jackson closed his notebook and looked down at his watch.

"Oh no! My mum is going to kill me," he cried, grabbing his bag. "I was meant to be home an hour ago."

"Do you need a lift? I can ask my dad?" I asked as he rushed past me.

44

"No, I'll be fine. I'll knock on you tomorrow," he shouted back as he ran through the trees. "Bye Tyler, Bye Shona."

We both said our goodbyes, but he'd already vanished out of view.

"He's a bit of a strange one," Shona laughed.

"Yeah, but he seems nice," I replied. "And all that research he's done, it's mad."

"I know, right." She turned to me. "Listen, me and a few friends were going to hang out a little later tonight if you fancy it?"

"I can't," I said. "My parents will kill me if I stay out too late."

"Are you sure? It'll be a good laugh."

I was tempted, like really tempted, but getting grounded wouldn't be the best way to spend my first week in Lochview.

"Another time," I promised.

"OK, I'll hold you to that." She smiled. "I'll catch up with you tomorrow then, yeah?"

"Definitely."

With a small wave, she walked off into the trees. I stood for a minute staring out over the water. Maybe, out there somewhere, the Lady of the Loch was staring back.

The thought sent a cold shiver down my spine.

I grabbed my bag and made my way back through the wood.

As I came back down the road, I saw Dad out front fixing the garden fence.

"Here he is," he called out to me. "The wanderer returns. How was the tour?"

"It was good," I said, standing behind him as he straightened one of the posts.

"It must have been a pretty long tour if you're only just getting back now." He reached down for his tool bag.

"I met some people while I was there," I told him. "We headed down to the loch when it was finished."

Dad stopped and looked up at me with a smile.

"Good. I'm glad you're making friends." He straightened up and placed his hand on my shoulder. "See, maybe Lochview isn't all bad."

He was right.

I'd had a really good day, and spending time down at the loch with Jackson and Shona was actually kind of fun.

Maybe, just maybe, Lochview was starting to grow on me.

11

"She's coming for you, and she won't rest until she has taken your soul."

I sat up in bed. My TV lit up the room, playing some cheesy old black-and-white horror movie. I must have left it on when I fell asleep.

I chuckled to myself and grabbed the remote. Though turning it off left the room in darkness.

I reached over to my bedside table and fumbled blindly for my phone. I found it and raised it to my face.

01:00am

With a groan, I rubbed my eyes and put it back.

Tap.

I froze. I waited in the dark to hear the noise again, but there was nothing. After a couple of seconds, I rested my head on the pillow. Maybe I'd just imagined it.

Tap.

OK, I definitely hadn't imagined it. Something was tapping at my window.

With a click, I turned on my lamp and climbed out of bed. As I stood facing the window, its curtain rustled gently in the breeze. Taking a deep breath, I reached out.

I felt its thick, rough fabric in my hand and pulled it aside.

Nothing.

Outside the window, there was nothing but the night sky. The moon and stars shone brightly against the blackness. I let out a sigh of relief and turned back to my bed.

"Tyler!"

I stopped and went back. Looking down I saw a familiar mop of red hair nestled in amongst the bushes.

"Shona, what are you doing?" I called down in a loud whisper.

"I came to get you, everyone's heading down to the loch."

"I told you earlier, I can't come out." I looked back over my shoulder, hoping that no one else was awake.

"I know, but I chose to ignore that." She shrugged. "You'll learn, it's something I do a lot."

I thought for a moment. There was no sound from the rest of the house. Maybe I could pull this off.

"OK, give me a minute."

Grabbing some clothes, I quickly got changed. For a moment I just stood in the middle of my room, staring at the door.

You can do this.

I'll be honest, it was my first time sneaking out in the middle of the night and I was more than a little terrified.

I opened my bedroom door painfully slowly, gritting my teeth as I begged it not to creak.

I stepped out and tiptoed across the landing. Holding my breath as I passed my parents' door.

Under the cover of darkness, I snuck down the stairs and into the kitchen. I picked up my shoes from beside the door and pulled out a chair at the table.

A jolt of excitement ran through my body. It looked like I was actually going to pull this off.

Creak.

The excitement turned to panic. I could hear footsteps on the landing above me. Someone was coming downstairs.

I was busted, there was no way I could explain why I was sitting in the kitchen, fully dressed at one in the morning.

I had to do something.

I had to hide.

I looked frantically around the room, but every nook and cranny was filled. Whether it was pots and pans, plates and bowls, or even the mop and bucket, everything had found a home and there was no space for me anywhere.

Except for under the table.

I dropped to my knees and clambered underneath, tucking my chair in tightly behind me.

Click.

The light came on and I held my breath. From my secret spot, I spied Dad's slippers standing in the doorway. He shuffled across the kitchen to the sink, I heard the clink of a glass as he turned on the tap and poured himself a drink.

Lying on the floor I felt a slow tingle slowly crawl along my arm, at first I thought it was nerves, but then I saw the long spindly legs of a spider creep across the back of my hand. The hand that was only inches from my face.

I bit my lip, trying hard not to scream.

I could feel its beady little eyes watching me as I resisted the urge to freak out. Dad was still by the sink, and I knew if I made the slightest noise, it was game over.

Each passing second felt like an eternity.

Finally, he moved, slowly walking back towards the living room. I could feel my body starting to shake as I closed my eyes and begged for him to hurry up.

There was another click and the room went dark.

I shook my hand, sending my unwanted friend flying across the room. Once I heard Dad's steps reach the top of the stairs I climbed out from under the table and dusted myself off.

Silently I unlocked the front door and turned the handle. With a huge sigh of relief, I stepped out into the cold night air.

Glancing back at the cottage, I smiled. I had escaped, and my family didn't have a clue.

I headed around the back of the house and found Shona sitting by the edge of the water.

"You made it then?" she said. Looking around at me.

"Just about. Where's everyone else?" I asked.

"They're waiting for us." She climbed to her feet. "Come on, let's go."

"Where are we going?" I started to feel nervous. I was sneaking out in the middle of the night with a girl that I'd only met that afternoon. It all seemed a bit crazy.

"Just trust me." There was a real excitement in her eyes. "We're going somewhere that will blow your mind."

12

"Is it much further?" I asked, trudging through the mud.

We'd been walking for ages. Shona had led me far beyond Jackson's secret cove. We'd gone so deep into the woods that I couldn't even see the night sky through the trees. No stars, no moon, just blackness.

"Stop complaining," she called back to me. "You said you wanted to find the Lady of the Loch. Well, you're not going to find her in the daytime."

I stopped.

"Hang on, I thought you said we were meeting your friends?" I asked.

"Why can't we do both?" She grinned. "Come on, it's just through here."

There was something in her smile that unsettled me, for a moment I considered turning back, but we'd been walking for so long that I wasn't sure I could find the way. So instead, I just followed, quietly worrying that this was a terrible idea.

The ground started to slope down towards the loch, and as we got closer to the water, I could hear voices ahead.

"Hey guys, say hello to Tyler," Shona announced as she stepped onto a small pebble beach.

The group went silent as I stood beside her. I could feel their eyes turn to me.

"Hi," I said nervously.

"This is Jay, over there is Charlie and these are the twins, Lucy and Fran," she said. "Everyone, this is Tyler."

For a moment no one moved, I felt awkward and didn't really know what to say. Then Jay stepped forward and shook my hand.

"Pleasure to meet you," he smiled.

He was slightly taller than I was, with long black hair and dark brown eyes. I'd have guessed that everyone else was around my age, but Jay seemed a little older.

Once Jay had greeted me the twins seem to relax.

"You've just moved here, right?" Fran asked. She and her sister looked identical, with blonde curly hair and big blue eyes. They both wore large hoop earrings and puffer jackets. "Where did you live before?"

"Yeah, where are you from?" Lucy chipped in, they even sounded identical.

"I'm from Oxford," I replied. "I just moved here a couple of days ago."

"An English boy?" Fran giggled.

"That explains why you sound so posh," Lucy added.

I didn't know what to say. If there was one thing that I definitely wasn't, it was posh.

"Are you not going to come and say hello, Charlie?" Shona shouted over to the boy standing silently by the loch. With his baby face and mousy brown hair, Charlie looked to be the youngest of the group.

"Don't worry about him," Jay said. "He can take a while to warm up to new people."

"So, Tyler here is investigating the Lady of the Loch," Shona told them, placing her hand on my shoulder.

Suddenly everyone was looking at me again, but this time there was excitement in their eyes and smiles on their faces. Everyone except for Charlie that is, I thought I saw him glance over for a split second, but in the blink of an eye he was back to standing like a statue, looking longingly out over the water.

"We should take him to the island," said Fran and Lucy almost in sync.

"That's exactly what I was thinking," Shona said.

As she turned to me, I felt my stomach drop.

"What's on the island?" I asked.

"The graves of all those taken by the Lady of the Loch." Everyone turned and faced Charlie, he was the last person I expected to answer my question.

"I thought her victims went missing?" I said, confused. "How could they bury their bodies if they couldn't find them?"

"They didn't. It's just their names carved into the stones." Jay replied. "But that's where it gets interesting, because you won't find it on any map, and no one knows who wrote the names."

"What do you say? You want to check it out?" Shona was looking at me eagerly.

In fact, they all were. I kind of wished Jackson was there. A genuine clue about the Lady of the Loch, he'd have loved this.

"Maybe we should wait until tomorrow, we could invite Jackson along." As the words left my mouth, I could see the disappointment on Shona's face.

"Oh, yeah you're totally right," she said. "Sorry, I didn't even think, of course we shouldn't go without Jackson."

"It's not your fault," I said, trying to comfort her.

"No, I got carried away." Shona turned her back to the group and leant in towards me. "Listen, I only met these guys the other day and I just thought it might be cool if we all did something together. But it's fine, we'll wait."

I felt the energy vanish from the group. It was like I'd just sucked all the fun and excitement out of everyone.

"You know what? Forget it. Let's do it," I said, flashing Shona a smile. "We'll just tell Jackson about it when we see him tomorrow."

Immediately the buzz was back, and everyone got to their feet. Jay led the way following the edge of the loch.

"Thank you," Shona whispered in my ear, before running off after the twins.

As we moved along the beach Charlie came and walked by my side.

Whilst the others chatted away in front of us, he turned to me, speaking in a hushed voice.

"You should be careful," he said. "Not everyone who goes to the island makes it back alive."

13

We hadn't been walking long when the island came into sight. It was small and overgrown with thick bushes and trees, sitting in the water not far from the shoreline. Jay walked us further along the beach until we reached an old rickety wooden bridge.

With its planks rotten and broken, and one of the handrails fallen away, it looked ready to collapse at any moment.

"Who's going first then?" I asked, hoping they weren't going to say it was me.

"I'll go," Jay volunteered, stepping out onto the first plank. "Don't worry it's sturdier than it looks."

The twins followed next, practically skipping across, then Shona. Leaving just me and Charlie.

"After you," he said, pushing me towards the bridge with a creepy grin.

"Thanks," I replied sharply. I don't know what I'd done, but I was getting the feeling he wasn't my number one fan.

I placed my foot delicately on the bridge. It creaked slightly but held firm. Slowly I concentrated on putting one foot in front of the other.

I could see the loch's inky waters through the gaps in the bridge. For a moment I wondered just how deep it was, like if I was to fall in now, how far down would I go?

The thought sent a shiver down my spine, but I shook it off and pressed forward.

The end was in sight. I could see Jay and the twins waiting with Shona.

"Come on, we've not got all night." Shona laughed.

Crack!

As I placed my foot down, I instantly knew something was wrong.

With an almighty crash, the plank snapped beneath me. I fell down hard, going through the bridge and plummeting into the water below.

It was as cold as ice. I kicked hard, trying to fight my way back to the surface but instantly my legs felt heavy. My arms reached upwards, desperately trying to grab onto something, anything that could save me.

But there was nothing.

The more I struggled the harder it got to move. No matter how much I fought I could feel myself sinking deeper and deeper into the darkness.

A hand!

I felt their fingers clasp around my wrist as I was pulled upwards. With renewed strength I kicked one last time, driving myself up and out of the water.

With a cough and a splutter, I landed on the beach.

Looking up I realised I was surrounded by a scattering of gravestones, all in different shapes and sizes, nestled between bushes and trees. They were each covered in names, but not neatly carved as you'd expect. Instead, it was like someone had scratched them into the stone.

"Tyler, are you OK?" Shona was leaning over me, her arm wet from where she had grabbed me.

"Thank you," I stuttered, shivering from the cold.

Fran and Lucy took off their jackets, wrapping them around me.

"I'm so sorry, maybe you were right, maybe we should have just come back tomorrow," Shona said.

"It's fine," I replied. "You weren't to know the bridge would break, and anyway, if it wasn't for you, I'd have been a goner, you saved my life."

"I guess I kind of did," said Shona. "Does that mean you owe me now?"

"Well, that depends on what you want." I laughed.

"I'm sure I'll think of something." Shona smiled, helping me to my feet.

As I wiped a lump of mud from my knee, I noticed something out of the corner of my eye.

Sat resting under a thick bush was a small green leather notepad.

I knew it was Jackson's before I even picked it up, but it was as I opened the cover that my heart stopped.

Scrawled across the front page was a message. A message for me.

Tyler, if you're reading this, RUN!!!

14

I had to get out of there. I'd seen how Jackson had clutched to his notebook, there was no way he was going to leave it behind unless he really had to, unless he was in real danger.

"Isn't that Jackson's?" Shona asked, a worried look on her face. "Do you think he's OK?"

"I'm sure he's fine." I smiled back at her, quickly closing the book. "Listen, we should probably be heading back, it's getting late. My parents will go mental if they realise I've snuck out."

"But we only just got here." Jay laughed. "Maybe your friend is still here. We should find him and say hi."

"He isn't," I said forcefully. "I just really think we should get out of here, like now."

Shona turned to me, lowering her voice.

"Are you OK? You're acting strange," she said, placing her hand on my back.

"I don't want to panic anyone," I whispered. "Jackson left me a note."

I opened the book for her to see. Her eyes widened.

"OK, let's get going guys," she said, turning to the group. "Tyler's soaking, we need to get him back home in the warm."

There were moans and groans but eventually everyone headed back towards the bridge. Everyone except Charlie. He looked around shiftily and said he was going to stay for a little longer.

"Thank you," I said to Shona as the others passed by.

"It's cool," she replied. "It's what friends are for."

Once we reached the shoreline everyone went to split off in different directions. Shona offered to walk me home, which was lucky because there was absolutely no hope of me finding my way in the dark.

We said our goodbyes to the rest of the group and set off.

The sun was just starting to rise as we came to the edge of the wood. Shona stopped before we stepped out into the open.

"I better be going," she said. "I'm in the other direction."

"Thank you." I shuffled my feet awkwardly. "Listen, pulling me out of the loch, helping get everyone moving. I really can't thank you enough."

"Don't mention it." She smiled. "Like, really don't, it's just awkward."

We both laughed.

"Do you think Jackson is OK?" I asked.

"I guess we'll just have to wait and see. We can head back tomorrow in daylight."

"Sounds like a plan."

Shona headed back into the trees and I turned for home, but as the old shabby cottage came into view my stomach twisted into knots.

All the lights were on.

Tucking Jackson's notebook under my jacket I marched on, ready to accept my fate. As my hand touched the cold metal of the door handle, I braced myself for the punishment that awaited me on the other side.

But it never came.

Instead, as I opened the door, my parents rushed towards me, throwing their arms tight around me.

"Tyler!" Mum cried. "Where have you been? We were so worried."

"Why are you all wet?" Dad asked, concerned.

"I just went out with some friends," I replied. "We were messing around and I slipped into the loch. I'm sorry."

"It's OK," Mum said, coming in for another hug.

Looking over her shoulder I was hit by a sudden wave of confusion. Sitting opposite my sister at the table was a very unexpected guest.

He wore a very smart grey tweed suit, but looking down I noticed spatters of mud at the bottom of his trouser leg. I guess I hadn't been the only one on a late-night walk.

"What's Archie doing here?" I blurted out.

"Don't be rude, Tyler," Mum scolded. "He was worried about you."

That didn't make sense. Why would he be worried about me? He didn't even know that I'd snuck out.

"I'm afraid I'm the bearer of bad news," he said, offering the seat next to him. "The young man you left the manor with earlier..."

"Jackson?" I said.

"Yes." Archie paused, there was an awkward silence. "I'm sorry to say, Jackson is missing."

15

After Archie left, I went to bed. I knew I wouldn't sleep but I didn't know what else to do.

Jackson was missing.

It didn't feel real. I'd spent all afternoon with him down by the loch and now he was gone.

Maybe it wasn't a coincidence.

We talked for hours about the Lady of the Loch, and then he goes missing and I find his notebook only metres away from the graves of her victims. A chilling thought crossed my mind.

What if she had returned?

Everything was getting way too real. Yesterday the Lady of the Loch was a fun story, a creepy legend I could investigate, but now everyone could be in real danger. If she took Jackson, then who would be next? Shona? Shona's friends? Me?

I'd been there with Jackson. I'd looked around the manor, I'd read his notes, I'd seen the island. Maybe I already knew too much.

Eventually, I drifted off, but I must have woken up two or three times throughout the night.

It wasn't until lunchtime that Mum appeared at my door.

"How are you feeling?" she asked, sitting on the end of my bed.

"I'm OK," I lied. I mean how could I be? There could be a child-stealing ghost on the loose and, for all I knew, I was her next victim.

Not that I could say any of that to my mum.

"We're all going to head into town," she said. "Why don't you come along?"

I didn't really have a choice in the matter. Before I even had a chance to answer Mum grabbed some clothes from my wardrobe and threw them at me.

"Come on, get yourself up and dressed. We're leaving in ten." She left and closed the door behind her.

I stretched and rolled out of bed as I heard her footsteps running down the stairs.

I quickly got myself ready and met everyone at the car.

Outside it was cloudy and grey. I pulled my coat tight around me, trying to fight against the chill in the air.

"Let's get going," Dad said as he climbed into the front seat. "We've got a lot to get done today."

"Well, we could have started earlier if someone hadn't snuck out last night," Emily said under her breath. I knew she wanted me to react, but I bit my tongue. I wasn't going to give her the satisfaction.

As we drove up the road, I turned back to look at the manor.

A cold tingle ran down my neck.

At a window on the second floor, I saw Archie's face staring back at me.

Watching as we drove away.

We arrived in Lochview to find the high street deserted. Other than an old couple wrapped up in heavy coats, walking a small fluffy dog, there seemed to be no one around.

Dad turned off the main road and parked up outside the café.

As he unlocked the front door, I noticed a girl walking down the street, a large pile of paper in her arms. She stopped at a shop across the road and stuck one of the sheets to the window.

My heart sank.

MISSING.

It was a missing person poster for Jackson. The photo looked like it had been taken on school picture day. He sat smiling in his uniform, his eyes big and bright behind those round glasses.

"Hey, excuse me!" The girl shouted.

I snapped back to the real world, she was running across the road towards me, her black braids bouncing loosely under a pink bobble hat.

"Hey, sorry. Is there any chance I could put one of these up in your window?"

I opened my mouth to speak, but Mum got there first.

"Of course," she said. "Anything we can do to help."

"Thank you." The girl handed her a poster.

"Did you know him well?" Mum asked.

"He's in my year at school," she replied. "Up at Cally Woods."

"Caledonian Woods?" Mum turned to me and my sister. "These two are starting there after the holidays. This is Emily, and this is Tyler."

"Nice to meet you. I'm Kaya." She smiled. "Anyway, I better get going. If you guys really are interested in helping, there is a group heading out later to look for Jackson. There's a number on the bottom of the poster."

"Of course, we'll be there." Mum nodded.

Kaya carried on down the street. Sticking posters anywhere she could find a space.

Mum placed ours in the window of the café.

All afternoon I kept looking back at it.

Silently hoping he could still be found.

16

"You're not going."

"But Mum..."

"No. That is my final say on it."

Mum had put her foot down, and I'd been in that position enough times to know there was no way she was going to budge. "Tyler, I'm sorry but it's just not for children."

I let out a frustrated groan. What if it was me that had gone missing? I bet she'd want everyone that could to be out there searching.

"Listen to your mother, Tyler," Dad said, lacing up his boots.

"I'll stay with you the whole time," I pleaded. "Dad, I can help."

"I know you can," he replied. "But your mum is right. Listen, I'm going to head out there with Archie and if we can find Jackson we will. I know you're worried, but the safest place for you is staying here with your mum and your sister."

I wanted to scream, I want to shout, I wanted to tell them they were being stupid, but there was no point.

I was never going to win.

"Why don't we put on a film?" Mum offered. "Try and take your mind off it."

I crossed my arms. As if watching a film was going to make anything better.

"I'm going to my room," I muttered and walked away.

Safe behind my bedroom door I started to throw things in a bag. A torch, a jumper, Jackson's notebook. They could try and keep me locked up here, but it wasn't going to work. The moment their backs were turned, I was getting out of there.

I was going to find Jackson.

With or without their permission.

I could hear Mum and Emily talking in the living room, then the TV took over. They must have decided to watch a movie after all. I felt my lips curl into a smile, that gave me a chance.

Backpack in hand, I silently snuck out of my room.

Looking down from the top of the stairs I could see the living room in darkness, Mum always closed the curtains to really get the cinema feel. With the windows covered, the only light came from the flickering screen.

The sofa faced away from the staircase, so if I could just make it past without making a single noise I was in the clear.

Slowly I made my way down. Carefully placing my foot on each step, I could only hope that they didn't creak.

There was a thudding in my chest, as I approached the bottom. I was so close, I just had to get around the corner and into the kitchen.

"I'm going to check your brother's OK," Mum said, pausing the film.

I froze.

Closing my eyes I held my breath, bracing myself for the inevitable.

"What's the point?" Emily replied. "He's just going to sulk up there. Leave him to it."

There was a silence. It felt like an eternity.

Please don't turn around.

"You're right," she said. "He'll come down when he's ready."

The TV kicked back into action and I breathed a sigh of relief.

I didn't say it often, but in that moment, I really loved my sister.

I made a break for the safety of the kitchen, just in case Mum changed her mind.

I quickly threw my shoes on, slipped out the front door and closed it softly behind me.

Outside it was still grey and miserable, with an icy chill in the air. Not that there was time to worry about that, I had a mission, and it was time to get moving.

First stop on my list, Jackson's secret spot by the loch.

I walked quickly towards the cover of the wood, constantly looking back over my shoulder to make sure no one had seen me.

After battling through the trees and bushes I found myself on the small beach where only yesterday me and Jackson had sat discussing the mysteries of the loch and the lady that haunted it.

Walking up to the water's edge, I wondered if he was out there somewhere, lost beneath its depths.

Deep down I hoped he'd be here, waiting for me, ready to tell me about all the new secrets he'd discovered.

But he wasn't. It was just me, standing alone.

I was just about to leave when I heard a voice.

"You're late."

17

"Shona?"

"The one and only." She smiled.

"What are you doing here?" I was confused, she was the last person I expected to find.

"The same as you, I'd imagine," she said, sitting on the same log Jackson had perched himself on yesterday. "I heard about Jackson. Half the town are out looking for him."

"Yeah I know, my dad is out here somewhere with my neighbour Archie."

"Archie Macleod?" she asked. She seemed surprised.

"Yeah," I said. "You know him?"

"Everyone knows him." She laughed. "He's Mad Man Macleod. I swear the only way he could be more excited about ghosts is if he was one. Honestly, the guy kind of gives me the creeps. Living alone in that big old house, it's weird."

"What do you mean?"

"He's just the caretaker, but he struts around like he owns the place. I'm just saying it's a bit strange. I always thought he was hiding something in there." She raised an eyebrow. "Like the bodies of the real owners."

I ignored Shona's crazed smile, but she was right about one thing. There was something strange about Archie.

Something beyond his odd fashion sense, if you could even call it that. He seemed to have an unnerving habit of popping up. Last night at my house, this afternoon at the window as we drove away, it felt like he was always there, always watching.

"What if he is hiding something?" I said.

"Like what?" she asked.

"I don't know," I replied. "When I first met Jackson, he was at the manor looking into the Lady of the Loch. What if he went back there last night? What if Archie caught him snooping around?"

An image popped into my head. Archie sat at the table in our kitchen. His suit was perfect, but for the specks of mud at the bottom of his trouser leg. Mud that he could have picked up whilst disposing of a certain book-shaped piece of evidence.

I reached into my bag and pulled out Jackson's notebook. I turned past his haunting message on the front page and flicked through to the end.

His final entry had a list of names scrawled messily down the page. Edward Mackenzie, Charles Dowell,

James Galloway, the list went on. Then underneath, I found what I was looking for.

She lived in the manor.

"Shona, look at this," I said, holding the book out to her. "He went up to the house last night, I know it."

"So what do we do?" she asked.

"I say we retrace his steps." I could feel myself getting excited. "Half the town are out here looking for Jackson, if he's near the loch, they're going to find him. We need to think outside the box, try something different, and I think the manor is the perfect place to start."

"OK," she said. "I'm in."

I put the notebook back in my bag and led the way. I pushed through the bushes and branches as if they were nothing. We were on a mission, and I wasn't going to let anything stand in our way.

I was so busy pushing ahead that it took a minute for me to notice that Shona had stopped.

"Did you hear that?" she asked.

"Hear what?" I turned back to see her frozen to the spot.

Listening carefully, I heard the rustle of leaves, but there was nothing to be seen.

"We should keep moving," I whispered.

Shona nodded, and we started creeping forward. Carefully checking each and every shadow for the source of the noise.

Snap!

A twig hit the ground just in front of me. Slowly I lifted my head.

Perched above me was a large bird. Its sharp talons wrapped firmly around the branch. Its piercing yellow eyes stared at me, unblinking.

"What is that?" I could hear the nerves in Shona's voice.

"It's a Peregrine Falcon," I said. "There's a sculpture of one in the manor."

"OK, well what do we do?"

It was a good question. Falcons were natural predators, I knew that much from school, and being face to face with one now I discovered they are much larger in person.

It shuffled its claws on the branch and dipped its head. As it stretched its wings wide, I was starting to realise it was even bigger than I thought.

"Tyler, what is it doing?" Shona asked, I felt her hand on my shoulder.

"Just stay perfectly still."

I didn't know if it would work but it felt like the right thing to say.

"Jackson!"

It was a man's voice, coming from somewhere out in the woods. The falcon tucked in its wings and raised its head.

"Jackson, are you out there?"

With a hard flap of its wings the bird dove from its perch and took off through the top of the trees.

I breathed a heavy sigh of relief. I turned to see Shona trying to catch her breath.

"Come on," I said. "We best get going."

I couldn't risk being caught outside the house.

We hurried through the rest of the forest until we found ourselves back at the road. In front of us, the manor stood dark and menacing against the setting sun.

I paused for a moment, checking to make sure there was no one else around, and then waved Shona on as we ran to the front door.

I wrapped my fingers around the heavy iron handle and turned.

It wouldn't budge.

"It's locked," I said, turning to Shona.

I guess it shouldn't have been a surprise. I knew that Archie was out, of course he would lock the front door.

"Look down there." Shona pointed past me, along the wall of the manor, to an open window.

I followed her along the outside of the house. In the time it took me to look back over my shoulder she had already slipped inside.

I'd like to say I climbed through the window expertly and with ease, but the truth is it was more a cross between a tumble and a fall. Regardless of how it happened though, I was inside.

"What are you doing down there?" Shona giggled.

She reached out and offered me a hand, pulling me up to my feet.

I had landed in the drawing room. I remembered it from Archie's tour. Two green leather sofas sat facing each other in front of a large stone fireplace.

"Let's take a look around," I said.

The wooden floorboards creaked softly as I moved out into the hallway.

I looked from one end to the other, unsure of which way to go.

"Do you want to know a surefire way to find out where someone is hiding something?" Shona asked, stepping past me.

She began to walk down the hallways, opening doors a crack and then closing them again.

"OK," I replied, a little confused.

"All you have to do is look for the locked door."

Click.

She stood with a smug look on her face.

"But how do we open it?" I asked. "We don't have a key."

"Who needs a key?" She reached into her pocket and pulled out a paper clip. "While you were busy rolling around on the floor, I found this."

Shona intricately uncurled the paperclip into two prongs. She slipped them into the lock and with a small wiggle and a twist the door swung open.

"Show off," I muttered under my breath as I followed her into the room.

It was a small office. A dark wooden desk sat by the window, next to it a wall of bookcases stretched high, filled with thick hardcovered books.

A black bowler hat hung on a stand by the door. Yet somehow it felt out of place. I couldn't imagine Archie wearing it, it didn't seem crazy enough.

"Tyler, I think you better look at this." There was a note of fear in Shona's voice that unsettled me.

I joined her at the desk, and she handed me a paper file. At first glance, it seemed pretty ordinary. That was until I saw the label.

Tyler Buckland.

It was a file on me.

18

"I'll see you tomorrow."

I heard Archie's voice echo down the empty halls of the manor. I looked at Shona and she looked back, it was clear from her face that she was just as panicked as I was.

"Quick, we need to get out of here," she said, lowering her voice.

I turned to grab the folder, and by the time I turned back, she was gone. I looked down the hallway just in time to see her sneak back into the drawing room. She looked back and waved her hand, telling me to follow.

But I froze.

I could hear footsteps from down the hall.

They were coming my way.

I dove back into the room, closing the door gently behind me. I needed somewhere to hide.

In the corner, I spotted a door built into the wooden panels on the wall. I pulled the handle and revealed a cupboard full to the brim with boxes.

Desperately I looked for another option, maybe under the desk, or behind the door, but Archie's footsteps were getting closer by the second. The cupboard was going to have to do.

Climbing in, I twisted and squeezed my way around the boxes. Once inside I pulled the door closed behind me.

I was half sat, half crouched against the piles of boxes, all alone in the pitch black. The air was thick with dust and damp. I didn't even want to think how long the boxes had been there, let alone what might be inside.

I heard the footsteps come to a halt.

Click.

With a soft creak, the door to the study opened. I held my breath, trying my best to not make a sound. I could hear him slowly walk into the room.

I held the folder tight to my chest. He was going to notice it was missing, I could feel it. He would see it was gone and then know I was here.

A single bead of sweat ran from my forehead down the tip of my nose. I have never moved as carefully as I did to wipe it away with my hand.

I was starting to get uncomfortable. I could feel my left leg falling asleep. Whilst the dust in the air itched my eyes.

Please just go.

The thought was only in my head, but it seemed to work.

Archie's footsteps started moving away, and with a soft click, I heard the door shut behind him.

I waited a moment longer to make sure he was gone, and then cautiously I opened the cupboard door. Breathing a sigh of relief, I climbed out from behind the boxes and stretched my legs.

Slowly, I crept towards the door.

"Good evening, Master Buckland."

My heart gave a single thud.

Archie was leaning against the desk.

"I think you should take a seat," he said. I tried to subtly hide the folder behind my back, but it wasn't subtle enough. "Don't worry, there will be time to get to that later."

"What is it?" I asked, nervously.

"All in good time," Archie said, gesturing to the chair at the desk.

I hesitated. To say I was uncomfortable was an understatement. I wanted to run, but where would I go? It's not like I'd be hard to find; you could see my house from the window.

Keeping my eyes on my would-be captor the entire time, I made my way to the chair. Gripping tightly to the folder.

"Thank you," he said. "Tell me, is there anyone else hiding in the manor? Any accomplices I need to be aware of?"

"No," I lied. Hopefully by now, Shona had escaped. Maybe she was even running for help as we spoke.

Archie looked at me for a moment and then nodded.

"Good," he said.

Then pulled a small key from his pocket and locked the door.

19

"Perfect. Now we know for certain that we will not be disturbed." Archie placed the key back in his pocket and turned to face me. "Let's start with a simple question. What are you doing here?"

"Nothing," I said sheepishly.

"You broke into my home, Tyler, I'm afraid you are going to have to do a little better than that." He crossed his arms with a stern look.

"This isn't your home." The words fell out of my mouth before I even had a chance to think.

"Excuse me?" Archie replied.

"This isn't your home," I repeated. "You might walk around like you own the place, but you don't."

Archie let out a quiet laugh, but it was anything but happy.

"You are correct, Tyler. I do not own Lochview Manor," he said, carefully considering each word. "But let me tell you, just because I do not own this house, doesn't mean it's not my home."

A tense silence fell. I shifted nervously in my seat.

"I'm going to give you one last chance before I call your parents," Archie said. "What are you doing here, Tyler?"

The mention of my parents changed things. If Dad found out I'd snuck out again then you could forget about the Lady of the Loch, I'd be locked in my room for the rest of my life.

"I was looking for Jackson," I answered quietly.

"You think I took Jackson?" Archie genuinely looked surprised.

"Well, if not you then the woman," I said.

"What woman?" The look of surprise turned to concern.

"The woman in the window." As I spoke Archie's face went white as a sheet. "I saw her that first night when you were locking up. I was walking back home, and she was there, watching me."

"Tyler." He spoke slowly, his voice trembling. "There is no woman living here."

A chill ran through my body.

What did he mean there was no woman here? I'd seen her. She was real. She had to be.

Something changed in Archie's eyes.

"There is something I need to tell you. I wish it was under better circumstances but I have a feeling that time may be against us." He paused. "Why do you think you're here?"

"I just told you..." I replied, confused.

"No. Why do you think you're here?" he repeated. "Why Lochview? You were living in Oxford, a normal boy with a normal life. Why come to Lochview?"

"Because my parents bought a house here," I said. "I didn't have a choice."

"Exactly, you didn't have a choice." He looked at me like I should be starting to understand. "Perhaps your parents didn't either."

I was lost.

"What if I told you that you were always meant to come to Lochview?" he asked. "What if I told you it was your destiny?"

"Then I'd say you were crazy." It was the truth. I know Shona said that Archie was a little strange, but I was starting to think he could actually be insane. "Look, I'm sorry for breaking in, I know I shouldn't have done it, but I was just looking for Jackson. Please, if I give you back the folder will you let me go?"

"Tyler, you are part of something bigger than you could ever imagine. Fate brought you here and I can prove it." He pointed at the folder in my arms. "Open it."

For a moment I just stared at him, unsure of how to respond.

Slowly I turned and placed the folder on the desk. Nervously I opened the cover.

The first page was full of names, with scribbles and lines connecting them like a web. As I looked down I started seeing names I recognised, my grandparents, my aunts and uncles, my parents, my cousins, my sister and at the very bottom me.

"What is this?" I asked.

"That is your family tree," Archie replied. "It is also a list of the modern-day descendants of the Dowell family."

"The Dowell family?" I echoed. "As in Lord Dowell?"

"Yes, the entire long line of Lord Dowells, and not forgetting the Lady Dowells too." He smiled briefly. "Now, exciting as this may sound, there is something you need to know."

"Am I going to be rich?" I asked.

"Tyler, now is not the time—" he tried to reply, but I interrupted.

"And the manor, do we inherit the manor?" I was getting carried away, but who could blame me? Just imagine it, Lord Tyler Buckland. It had a ring to it.

"Tyler, you are in danger," Archie said forcefully. "The Dowells may have been Lords of Lochview but that wasn't all. Lochview isn't like other towns, throughout history it has borne witness to many things that cannot be explained. The Dowell family acted as its protectors against creatures and events that fell outside the realm of science and reason."

"What do you mean?" I shifted uncomfortably in my seat.

"I mean the supernatural." He paused for a moment. "People will tell you there are things in this world that cannot exist. Those people are wrong."

"The Lady of the Loch," I said, under my breath.

"Precisely." Archie looked at me with a grave expression. "Tyler, it is my belief that she has returned, and that she claimed her first victim last night. There is a power at Lochview that has brought you home. I have to believe that is for a reason, I think it is your destiny to stop her, once and for all."

I was speechless. I tried to say something, anything, but there were no words. Meanwhile, Archie just stared at me, waiting.

Finally, I broke the silence.

"I think I'd like to go home now." It was all too much. I just wanted to go to bed, close my eyes and forget any of this happened. Forget about Lochview, forget about Jackson, forget about the Lady of the Loch.

"OK. I understand, it's a lot to take in." Archie placed his hand on my shoulder, I could hear the disappointment in his voice. "But if you ever find yourself in trouble, just know that I am here to help."

"Thank you," I said softly.

Archie took the key out of his pocket and unlocked the door. With a soft click, I was free once more.

I followed him to the entrance hall.

Suddenly Archie stopped in his tracks.

"What is it?" I asked, looking round him.

I didn't need to wait for a response

A message had been scrawled across the large front doors, the letters dripping in red as if it was bleeding from the wood itself.

She has returned.

20

The soft sound of rain started pelting against the window.

"I think we should get you home." Archie's voice quivered as he spoke. "Just wait here a moment and I'll get my jacket."

Archie shuffled quickly into the next room. I stood transfixed, watching as the letters dripped slowly down the door.

She has returned.

Any doubt in my mind vanished in the blink of an eye. The Lady of the Loch was real, and that spelt danger.

Something stirred out of the corner of my eye. Something beyond the rain-speckled glass of the window. Something lurking in the darkness.

A face.

My heart stopped for a moment.

The messy blonde hair, the thin round glasses.

It was Jackson.

I stepped forward, opening my mouth to call his name, but he turned and ran.

"Tyler, wait!" Archie shouted, but it was too late.

I bolted out the door. The night air slapped me in the face with its cold, wet breeze. In the distance, I saw Jackson running towards the woods and I gave chase.

My feet sunk deep into the sticky mud as branches clawed and scratched at my face.

"Jackson, wait up," I shouted. "It's me, It's Tyler!"

But it didn't stop him. He just kept running.

As I ran along the edge of the loch, the rain was replaced by a thick mist. I could barely tell where the ground ended and the water began.

Out of nowhere, my foot hooked itself on a branch and I fell hard.

I was winded, lying coughing in the mud.

With a groan, I climbed back to my feet.

In front of me was the decrepit old bridge, beyond which lay the island, dark and eerie in the pale moonlight.

"Jackson, are you there?" I called out, but there was no response.

Cautiously I made my way across. I could hear the waters lapping beneath me as I clung on tightly to the handrail. I certainly wasn't going to make the same mistake as last time.

Slowly I crept through the gravestones, each overgrown with moss and weeds, climbing and spreading across the roughly scratched names.

"Jackson?" I could barely manage more than a whisper. I had a sinking feeling in my gut, it was telling me we weren't alone. "Please, Jackson. Everyone is worried about you."

There was a rustle in the tree above me.

Looking up I saw a familiar pair of beady yellow eyes, piercing through the darkness.

The falcon sat perched on a branch, staring intensely.

"What do you want?" I asked. "Are you trying to show me something? I don't understand. Why are you here?"

A few days ago I'd have felt ridiculous speaking to a bird, but I was ready to try anything. Not that it was any use.

The bird remained, unmoving on its branch.

"I thought you were meant to be some great messenger from the other side?" I could feel the frustration bubbling inside me. "Well come on then, what's the message? Where is Jackson?"

My foot hit something solid as I stepped forward. Losing my balance, I swung my arms like a windmill trying not to fall over. Looking down, I realised there was something buried beneath the mud.

Above me, there was a soft squawk, as the peregrine cocked its head.

"Is this what you wanted to show me?" I asked, crouching down.

I scraped away at the dirt and the moss, revealing a large flat stone underneath. Unlike the other stones, it had no name, just a small carving in its centre.

It was the image of a lion on a shield, surrounded by intricate patterns. The names scratched into the other stones looked rough and untidy, but this was neat, precise. Something inside me stirred, I was sure I'd seen this before. I ran my fingers across the stone, following the lines of the emblem.

Then I stopped in my tracks.

A blood-curdling scream rang out across the loch.

I stayed perfectly still and listened intently. I could feel my heart pounding in my chest.

"Help! Please, someone, help!"

It was a girl's voice, and she was clearly in trouble.

The falcon screeched as I jumped to my feet. Racing back to the bridge, I found a girl in the water, clinging on for dear life, her arms wrapped around its rotten wood.

As I reached out to grab her arm, I recognised the terrified face looking back at me. It was Kaya, the girl with the posters from town.

"Hold on," I said, gripping tightly. "I've got you."

I pulled with all my might, but something was wrong. It was like something was dragging her down, some hidden force beneath the water.

"Please!" She cried. "Don't let go."

"I won't" I grunted, but I could already feel her arm starting to slip through my fingers. Her face dipped lower and lower towards the water.

I was losing.

I couldn't save her.

I summoned every ounce of strength I had, I heard her cough as her mouth slipped beneath the water.

I... can't... hold...

I felt two strong arms wrap around me and tighten my grip.

"Pull!"

I had no time to think, I just did as I was told.

Kaya erupted from the water, crashing down onto dry land as we all fell backwards. I turned to my left to see Archie, holding his chest trying to catch his breath.

"Is everyone OK?" he asked, panting heavily.

"I think so," I replied.

Kaya lay still, but I could see her breathing.

"Don't you ever run off like that again, Tyler," Archie scolded.

"I'm sorry," I said.

"What were you thinking?" he continued, barely letting me get a word in edgeways.

"I thought I saw Jackson," I replied quietly.

Archie sighed.

"Well next time you don't go alone." His tone softened. "Is that understood?"

"Understood," I repeated.

"Good." He nodded, dusting himself off. "Now let's get you and this young lady back home safe."

I helped Kaya stand up and we made our way back to the woods.

Before we left, I took one last look back at the island.

Even in the darkness, I could make out the shape of the falcon as it took to the sky, leaving the swirling mists of the loch in its wake.

21

As the manor came back into view I turned towards home. Before I left, I made Archie promise not to tell my parents I had snuck out again.

I could tell he wasn't happy about it, but he eventually agreed.

I slipped back into the house to find it in darkness. Careful not to wake anyone I headed straight upstairs and to my room.

I lay on my bed, my mind racing. Trying to put the evening's events behind me, I closed my eyes and waited for sleep to take hold.

When the sun finally rose, there was a knock at my door.

"Come in," I groaned, rubbing my eyes.

I watched the door handle twist before opening to reveal my sister in the doorway.

"Mum told me to come wake you up," she said. "Breakfast is nearly ready."

"I'll be down in a sec," I mumbled, rolling over and burying my head in the pillow.

I waited to hear the click of the door as my sister left, but it never came.

"Tyler..." She hesitated a moment, considering her words. "Can we talk?"

There was a graveness in her voice that caught me off guard. I'd seen my sister be many different things, but this level of seriousness was new. I raised my head and turned to her.

"Yeah, sure, come in," I replied nervously.

Emily hovered awkwardly in the middle of the room, not knowing what to say or do. Eventually, she made the decision to perch on the desk. Her mouth bobbed open a couple of times as she searched for her words.

"Tyler, you know if you were ever in trouble you can talk to me, right?" she asked, concern casting a dark shadow across her face.

"Yeah, of course—" The words had barely left my lips before she interrupted.

"It's just that something seems different with you. Sneaking out of the house, arguing back, all this stuff with that boy who went missing...I don't know, it just feels like something's going on." She paused for a moment, before continuing with a deep sigh. "Mum and Dad won't say it, but we're worried about you."

"I'm fine," I lied.

I was far from fine. In fact, I was so far from fine, that fine was just a tiny dot in the distance to me. But what could I say? A boy I met was taken by a ghost that our neighbour believes I am destined to defeat because our family is apparently descended from some monster hunting Lords and Ladies?

She'd think I was crazy.

I would think I was crazy.

A small part of me already did.

"Are you sure?" She was clearly unconvinced. "Anything at all that you want to say, I'm here to listen."

"Honestly Em, I'm OK. I'm just getting used to this place, it's all a bit...different," I said forcing a smile.

"I'll see you downstairs then." Emily stood from the desk. "Just remember that if you ever need to talk about anything at all, I'm here."

"Thank you" I replied, sinking back into my pillow.

Emily made her way to the door and then stopped.

"Just one more thing," she said, turning back. "Where were you last night?"

I hesitated.

"I was right here." Even I could hear the trembling in my voice.

"That's strange," she mused. "Because Mum sent me up to check on you, but when I did, you weren't here."

"Emily—" I started, but she cut me off.

"I won't tell Mum and Dad, but you need to start telling the truth." She let her words hang in the air. "I'll see you at breakfast."

With that, she closed the door. I could hear my heartbeat racing in my ears.

My brain kicked into overdrive.

What do I do?

If I tell her the truth, she won't believe me, she'll tell Mum and Dad I snuck out and I'll be grounded from now until eternity.

But if I couldn't tell the truth, then there was only one thing for it, I needed a lie.

A really good lie.

Something that would get my sister excited.

Something that would send her gossip-obsessed brain into meltdown.

A stomach-churning thought popped into my head. As much as it killed me inside, I knew what I had to do.

Throwing on some clothes I headed downstairs. My head hung low as I took a seat by Emily at the table in the kitchen.

I glanced at the door and considered making a run for it, but I knew there was no point.

There was only one way out of this.

Mum and Dad were busy plating up breakfast, so I took my chance and turned to my sister.

"You want to know where I was last night?" I whispered.

"Obviously," she said, raising her glass to her mouth.

"OK." I knew I had to sell it, so I paused dramatically. "I was meeting a girl."

Emily nearly spat her drink across the table. Mum and Dad turned around as she held her chest, coughing and spluttering.

Before she had a chance to interrogate me further there was a knock at the door.

"Hello?" Archie's voice called from outside.

"Come in," Dad shouted back, putting plates down on the table.

As Archie bounded through the door, Emily leant in close to my ear.

"We'll talk about this later," she whispered. "I've got my eye on you."

Maybe my plan wasn't as foolproof as I thought.

"Good morning, all," Archie exclaimed, greeting everyone with a polite nod. "I do apologise for interrupting your breakfast, I can come back later if it's more convenient?"

"No, it's fine," Mum replied. "How are you?"

"I'm very well, thank you." He smiled. "I shall keep it brief. I am in need of some assistance with a few tasks around the manor and I wondered if I could possibly enlist the services of young master Tyler."

My parents looked at each other, neither knowing what to say.

"Perhaps it could count as a punishment for his sneaking out the other night," Archie suggested. "I can assure you the jobs are certainly mundane enough."

"Actually, that would be great," Dad said. "We've got a lot of stuff to get through at the café, and it could be a late one."

I tried to open my mouth, but I couldn't get a word in.

"Perfect," he said, turning to me. "A pleasure to have you on board, Tyler. Be there at twelve o'clock sharp, and not a second later."

22

"Tyler, wait up."

I heard Shona's voice as I hurried up the road. As per usual, I was running late.

"I've got something to show you," she said, catching me up.

"I can't," I replied. "Archie has asked me to come up to the house."

"Woah, hang on." She grabbed my shoulder, stopping me in my tracks. "You're going to see Archie?"

"Shona, something happened last night, something big. Archie is...well...he's not who we thought." I glanced down at my watch. I was already five minutes late. "Why don't you come with me? You can see for yourself."

"Seriously?" She looked at me in disbelief. "Yesterday you thought he was involved in Jackson going missing."

"Well, I was wrong," I said. "He knows all about the Lady of the Loch, and I think he can help us stop her."

Silence hung in the air as Shona just stared at me.

"Listen, I need to go," I said tentatively.

"What if Jackson thought the same?" Shona asked.

"What?"

"What if Jackson thought that Archie could help him too, what if Jackson went there looking for answers, but it turned out to be a trap?" There was something different in her voice, it sounded like fear.

"Come with me then," I suggested "Let's solve this together."

"I can't." She shook her head. "I don't trust him, and I don't think you should either."

I looked up at the manor and then back to Shona. Her eyes glistened with tears.

"I'm sorry," I said. "I have to go."

"Fine, if you need me, I'll be down by the island." She turned and walked away.

I was torn. Part of me wanted to run after her, after all, we had started looking into the Lady of the Loch together, but at the same time, I couldn't ignore everything that happened last night. I needed answers, and right now I felt like Archie was the one who could help me find them.

Approaching the large wooden doors of the manor I raised my hand to knock, but before I could make contact the door opened in front of me.

"You're late," Archie said, looking down through the glasses at the end of his nose.

"Sorry, I was just chatting—" I started.

"It doesn't matter," he interrupted. "Come on through, we have a guest."

I paused for a moment as Archie scurried down the hallway.

A guest?

Quickly I followed after Archie. He stopped at the door to the drawing room and held it open for me.

Kaya sat on the green leather sofa by the fireplace. As I entered, she stood up.

"Miss Francis has been waiting for you," Archie said, closing the door behind us.

"I'm sorry," I stuttered. "I didn't realise you were here."

"It's OK," she replied, with a gentle smile. "I just wanted to thank you for last night. You saved my life."

"It was nothing," I said. "Anyone would have done the same."

An awkward silence hung in the air.

"Excellent, now that's out the way, maybe we should all take a seat." Archie nudged me in the back, his elbow pushing me towards the sofa. "I thought it may be helpful to discuss what happened last night, and more importantly how Miss Francis found herself in the loch."

"I don't remember anything." Kaya shrugged as I sat opposite her.

"Just take your time," Archie said. "What is the last thing you do remember?"

"I was in the woods looking for Jackson. It was getting dark so I was going to head home, but there was..." She stopped, her words trailing off.

"There was what?" I asked.

"No, it's nothing." She looked away. "You wouldn't believe me."

"Try us." I smiled, trying to reassure her.

She paused for a moment, then let out a sigh.

"I can't say for sure," she said. "But it looked like eyes staring at me through the mist."

"Yellow eyes?" I interrupted. "I've seen them too."

"No." She looked at me confused. "They were green. These green glowing eyes that felt like they were staring into my soul. They're the last thing I remember. The next thing I knew you were pulling me out of the water."

We all went silent. I turned to Archie, and he gave me an uncomfortable look.

"Kaya, what do you know about The Lady of the Loch?" he asked.

"The Lady of the Loch?" she repeated. "Like the story?"

"What if we told you it's not just a story?" he said.

She glanced between us and laughed.

"You're joking, right?"

Archie went over to the bookcase and skimmed his finger along the shelf, stopping at a small brown leather-bound book. He flicked quickly through the pages, and then all of a sudden he stopped and began to read.

"Her eyes burned green, two glowing spheres casting their evil through the mist. To look into those eyes was to surrender to the darkness that filled her soul." He slammed the book shut and looked up.

"What is that?" I asked.

"That is the witness account of one Isaac Mackenzie in eighteen twenty-three," Archie explained. "The only person known to have seen the Lady of the Loch and live to tell the tale. For a while at least."

"For a while?" I gulped.

"He disappeared two days later." Archie placed the book on the table between me and Kaya. "Miss Francis, I have no doubt that what you saw last night was the Lady herself, just as I have no doubt that she will come for you again."

Kaya looked at me, pure terror in her eyes.

"What do we do?" I asked.

Archie's reply was simple.

"We find a way to stop her."

23

"If there is a way to defeat her, it's in here."

Archie swung open the door to the library and instantly I was hit by the smell of old books. Inside shelves and bookcases climbed the walls from the floor to the ceiling, surrounding a large round table.

"Everything there is to know about Lochview is kept within these walls," he said, running his fingers along the line of leatherbound spines. "From journals to biographies, legends to case studies, everything known about her is documented in this room somewhere."

"There has got to be thousands of books in here," Kaya exclaimed. "Where do we even start?"

"You can start by grabbing a book," Archie replied.

We spent the afternoon turning through page after page, looking for anything relating to the Lady of the Loch. Sightings, victims, even rumours, if it had her name on it, we wanted to find it, but the more and more we looked, the more we found the same old stories we already knew.

As the sun started to set outside the window, we each collapsed into chairs around the room.

"This is hopeless." Kaya sat with her head in her hands.

"We just need something to point us in the right direction," Archie said.

We were all tired and on the brink of giving up when a thought hit me. I looked down at my backpack, resting against a pile of books on the floor.

"Actually, I might have an idea," I said.

They both turned and looked at me expectantly. I reached into my backpack and pulled out Jackson's notebook.

"What's that?" Archie asked.

"It's Jackson's. It's his notes on the Lady of the Loch," I explained, turning to the final page. "When I last saw him this page was empty. So—"

"So, these notes must be from the night he disappeared," Archie interrupted.

"Do these names mean anything to you?" I asked.

He thought for a moment and then leapt suddenly from his chair. Me and Kaya exchanged a glance as he rummaged wildly through piles of books in the centre of the table.

"Here!" He raised a large black book in the air. He mumbled to himself as he flicked through the pages. Suddenly he stopped and looked up. "Charles Dowell. Son of Lord William Dowell III. Born 17th January 1852, died 29th August 1863. No, wait..."

"What is it?" Kaya asked.

"There's no cause of death, it says he was missing." Archie looked up nervously.

Turning back through the notebook, I found the timeline recording all the known disappearances relating to the Lady of the Loch.

"Archie, I think he might be the first."

"The first what?" Kaya looked confused. "I don't understand."

"I think Charles Dowell was the first victim of the Lady of the Loch." There was an excitement building inside me. "What about the other names? Do we know anything about them?"

"Wait, I'll have a look." Archie closed his book and handed it to me, before turning back to the piles on the table. Kaya stepped forward to help him, leafing through books and piles of papers.

Glancing down at the book in my hands, my heart gave a thud.

The cover was blank, but for an emblem decorated in gold.

"Hang on," I said. "What's this on the cover?"

Archie looked down at the book and then back to me with a puzzled look.

"It's the Dowell family crest," he replied. "Why? Have you seen it before?"

Standing boldly against the dark leather was the golden outline of a shield, upon which stood a shimmering lion.

"The island where we rescued Kaya. There's a large stone rectangle with that mark on it." I felt a shiver run down my spine. "I think it was a grave."

"It can't be." He shook his head. "The Dowell family are buried at the church in town. There aren't any graves on the grounds."

"Well, I can only tell you what I saw," I said defensively. "Something is buried on that island."

"Hey, look at this," Kaya interrupted.

She held out a large book with glossy pages towards us. Inside was the portrait of a boy, sitting smugly with a green waistcoat over his white ruffled shirt.

My heart stopped.

Although the paragraph beneath the picture told me he was Charles Dowell, I knew he couldn't be. I knew it was impossible because Charles Dowell vanished in 1863, and I had spoken to the boy in portrait two nights ago.

It was Charlie.

"Tyler, are you OK?" There was concern in Kaya's voice.

"Are there more pictures?" I breathed deeply, I could feel my stomach churning.

She turned through the pages, past portraits of grand lords and ladies, each striking the same regal poses, and then I stopped her. The angelic faces of two young twins looked back at me, wide-eyed and smiling with their bouncing golden curls.

Francesca and Lucille.

A few pages further and there was Jay, except it wasn't, the book said his name was James Galloway.

As Kaya reached the final page, I could feel my hands shaking.

"I need to go," I said, grabbing my bag.

"Tyler, what is going on?" Archie looked at me, worried.

"Those faces, I've seen them before." My voice trembled.

"As in you've seen the portraits?" Kaya asked, but I could already see on Archie's face that he understood.

"You've met them in person," he said quietly.

"Two nights ago, down by the island." I nodded. "Listen, my friend Shona went there tonight and I think she might be in trouble. I'm sorry I have to go."

"I should come with you." Archie started towards me.

"No," I said, stopping him in his tracks. "You two stay here and find anything you can on banishing ghosts. If I'm right, we're going to need it."

24

I pulled my coat tight against the ice-cold rain.

As I ran through the darkness my mind was racing. Finally, I was starting to understand. The Lady of the Loch was a myth, that's why no one knew her name, why no one could find any record of her life or her story, because she was just that, a story. A legend made up by evil spirits to haunt Lochview.

But why?

What did they have to gain?

I pushed the questions from my head. There wasn't time, I had to concentrate on Shona.

As I reached the trees. I could already feel the guilt bubbling up inside me. I had let this happen, I let her go to the island alone.

What if I was already too late?

If they got to her first, then she was a sitting duck. She thought they were her friends, but this whole time they'd been lying to her.

Snap!

A tree branch snagged on my sleeve, tearing a hole in my coat. I felt a sharp pain followed by a warmth trickling down my arm.

I bit down on my lip, careful to not make a sound. Anyone could be lurking in the shadows, and the last thing I wanted was to draw attention.

I put my hand on the cut and pressed hard, it was something I'd seen in the medical shows my dad watched.

Slowly I got back to my feet. Through the last of the trees, I could see Loch Dowell, the moon casting an eerie light across its waters. Listening carefully, I heard nothing, everything lay silent, but for the gentle sound of the waves. So I cautiously stepped out into the open, keeping my eyes trained on the shadows, making certain I was alone.

I could feel my nerves growing.

I was starting to think this was a bad idea.

What if Shona had already left?

For all I knew she was sitting watching TV right now, complaining about how I'd ditched her, moaning to her parents about how terrible a friend I was.

But what if she wasn't?

It was a risk I couldn't take.

I made my way across the bridge, glancing around nervously, checking for even the smallest signs of movement.

I froze.

Ahead of me, a bush rustled gently. I told myself it was just the wind, but my gut disagreed.

I crept slowly towards it.

With each step, the fear grew inside me.

I was within touching distance when it rustled again, this time more aggressively than before.

I reached out.

I could feel the rough twigs in my hand as I went to pull it aside.

"Tyler?"

I nearly jumped out of my skin.

It was Shona. She stood behind me, a confused look on her face.

"What are you doing?" She asked.

"I thought I heard something," I replied, letting go of the bush.

"How was your afternoon with Archie?" She was glaring at me with her arms folded, clearly it was still a touchy subject.

"I'll tell you later," I said. "We need to get out of here."

"Why?" There was a stubbornness in her voice.

"We're in danger," I explained. "Shona, we found something big. Just come back to the manor and I'll show you."

"Actually, I found something too," she told me.

I could feel goosebumps creeping up my arm.

"OK, you can tell me about it when we're somewhere safe." I reached for her arm, but she pulled away.

"Or you could come take a look."

I hesitated for a moment, glancing back towards the bridge, but she was already walking away. I couldn't leave her again. So, I followed close behind.

She led me to an old gravestone. A large crack ran across it, filled with thick hairy moss.

Scratched into the stone were a series of names. Henry Dowell, Alexander Mackay, Isaac Mackenzie.

I stopped.

Suddenly I felt sick to my stomach.

At the bottom was a name I knew, freshly carved into the stone.

Jackson Weir.

25

I tried to speak but there were no words. I didn't know what to feel. Sad? Hurt? Angry? Maybe all of them at once. Not that it would make a difference.

He was gone.

Part of me had hoped that there was still a chance to save him, but seeing his name scratched into that stone like that was horribly final.

I turned to Shona.

"We need to go," I whispered, choking back a tear.

She opened her mouth to speak, but stopped and simply nodded.

We walked back to the bridge in silence. I think neither of us really knew what to say. As I went to take my first step onto the old creaking wood I hesitated.

"What's wrong?" she asked.

"The water," I said, staring down beneath my feet. "There's something in the water."

From the depths below me, I could see a small green light, flickering beneath the waves. Slowly it began to grow, spreading out across the loch.

I stepped back onto dry land as a thick mist started rolling in from all sides, lit by the glowing waters.

"Tyler, what's going on?" I could hear the panic in Shona's voice.

"It's going to be OK," I said. "Just stay close."

Fear was rising inside me. Across the bridge, I could see a silhouette stepping forward from the trees. A pair of green eyes burned brightly from the darkness.

I felt Shona's hand grab mine. Her skin was as cold as ice.

"It's her," she whispered, her voice trembling. "It's the Lady of the Loch."

"It can't be." I turned to her and looked her dead in the eye. "Shona, she's not real. She's just a story."

As the shadow came closer, I could make out the shape of a long flowing dress, and long hair blowing wildly in the wind.

I kept telling myself it wasn't her, it couldn't be, she wasn't real, but with every step she took, I began to doubt myself more and more.

What if I was wrong?

What if the Lady of the Loch was right there in front of me?

I looked around frantically, trying to find some means of escape, but there was nothing.

We were trapped.

We began to back away. Shona stood tight against my shoulder. The wet mud was heavy beneath my feet.

Then the figure stopped.

It just stood, staring with those haunting green eyes.

"Tyler," Shona squeezed my hand. "She's not alone."

Her words send a chill crawling slowly up my spine. As I looked out across the loch, I saw three more pairs of eyes shining through the mist.

An evil cackle echoed across the water as the figures walked slowly across the waves.

One by one they all began laughing, like hyenas circling their prey.

"I'm so sorry, Shona." A single tear ran down my cheek. "This is all my fault."

"No, it's mine. You wouldn't be here if it wasn't for me."

The figure in front of us stepped forward into the moonlight.

"You two should see your faces," said a familiar voice.

"Fran?" Shona stepped forward but I put my arm across her.

"Oh, come on, Tyler," Fran laughed. "Don't ruin our fun."

"Tyler? What's going on?" Shona gave me a confused look.

I glanced over my shoulder as Lucy, Charlie and Jay emerged from the mist. Walking effortlessly across the water.

"They're not who you think you are," I replied, slowly stepping backwards.

"Who are we then, Tyler?" Jay shouted as he stepped onto the island. "Or better yet, what are we?"

"Yeah, Tyler, tell her what we are." Lucy giggled. The sound of it made my skin crawl.

I could feel Shona staring at me.

"Tyler," she said. "Please, just tell me."

I took a deep breath and looked Jay in the eye.

"They're dead."

Once again, the sound of laughter rang out into the night. Their green eyes glowed brighter than ever as evil grins spread across their faces.

"We're so much more than dead," said Fran. "And you can be too. All you have to do is join us, Tyler."

They each reached out their right hand and slowly closed in on us.

"We don't want to join you," I cried out. "Just let us go."

I stumbled backwards as my foot caught on the edge of the large stone grave. I clambered back to my feet and looked Shona in the eyes.

This was it.

I could feel it in my gut.

Softly they started to chant under their breath.

"Join us. Join us. Join us."

I closed my eyes and thought of my family back at home. Mum and Dad were probably washing up in the kitchen, whilst Emily sat in front of the TV, all of them happily unaware they would never see me again. I didn't even have a chance to say goodbye.

Crack!

I felt a shift in the stone beneath my feet.

My heart gave a single thud.

Then with an almighty crash, I plunged into darkness.

26

I let out a groan.

Looking up from the cold stone ground I could see the moonlight shining across the uneven stairs I had just tumbled down. The air was thick with dust, I coughed as it caught the back of my throat.

"Shona?" I called out weakly, into the darkness.

There was no reply.

Slowly I climbed to my feet. My head was spinning as my eyes tried to adjust to the darkness. The room was largely empty, but for a huge stone crypt in the centre, its lid cracked and broken with age. I felt goosebumps crawl up the back of my neck as I realised where I was.

It was a tomb.

On the floor in front of me was a body, lying slouched and still amongst a pile of rocks.

"Shona?" I whispered. I placed my hands on her shoulders, shaking her gently. "Shona, can you hear me? Please, we need to get out of here."

"It's no use." Jay's voice echoed as he walked down the stone steps. Charlie and the twins followed close behind. "She's gone."

"No, she can't be." My voice cracked around the lump in my throat. "Shona? Come on, wake up. Please, wake up."

"There's no point even trying," said Lucy teasingly. "There's nothing you can do for her."

"Well, that is unless..." Fran trailed off. "No, there's no way he'd even consider it."

"Not a chance," Lucy agreed.

The two of them started cackling like a pair of witches. Their evil laughter filled the room. I looked down at Shona's limp body.

"What do I have to do?" I said, rising to my feet.

The room went silent.

"We can bring her back," said Charlie, his face cold and expressionless. "For a price."

A chill ran through my body.

"What do you want?" I asked.

"Nothing much." He smiled. "Just your soul."

The others chuckled softly.

I knew there was nothing I could do. There was no escape for me, but at least she maybe had a chance.

I took a deep breath.

"OK."

"Very well," Charlie said, his face twisting into an evil smile. "Then let us begin."

With a click of his fingers, a series of wooden torches around the room burst into flames. Their flickering light cast dancing shadows across a large star carved into the floor, with each of its five points linked in a circle.

Jay and the twins stepped forwards, taking Shona's lifeless body in their arms they lifted her onto the crypt. I watched helplessly, as they lay her body down, before each taking a position at a point of the star.

"What is this?" I asked.

"A pentagram," Charlie explained. "To most, it is simply a symbol of the dark arts, but to the enlightened, it is a gateway, a path to unimaginable power."

I felt sick. I looked at each of their faces, all smiling back at me. I wanted to run but there was nowhere to go.

"I can't do this," I said, shaking my head.

"No one is forcing you to do anything," Jay reasoned. "The decision is entirely your own. Either take your position and save your friend or refuse and share her fate."

I stood silent. Scared and afraid. There was only one thing I could do. I had no choice.

I hung my head, and I stepped forward.

Squawk!

Everyone turned towards the stairs. The screech of a bird echoed around the room.

In the pale moonlight, I could see the shadow of its wings stretching down the steps, but as it moved it twisted and contorted until it resembled the shape of a person.

The sound of beating wings was replaced with footsteps, descending into the tomb. I couldn't believe my eyes.

"Jackson?"

It just fell out of my mouth. I couldn't believe it. He was right there, right in front of me, clear as day. The messy blonde hair, the thin round glasses, it was really him.

"Tyler, don't listen to them!" he shouted, pushing past Charlie. "It's all a lie."

"But Shona—" I started.

"There's no time," he interrupted. "You need to go. Just trust me. They can't hurt you."

"Oh, I wouldn't be too sure about that," Fran laughed.

It didn't make sense. Of course, they could hurt me, he was evidence that they could hurt me. I'd lost him and I'd lost Shona to them, how could he possibly say they can't hurt me?

"Jackson, what is going on?" I asked under my breath.

"Tyler, listen," he hesitated. "Shona is..."

Then he stopped, his eyes opening wide.

"Shona is what?" I asked desperately.

I felt a cold breath on the back of my neck as Shona's voice whispered in my ear.

"I am the Lady of the Loch."

27

"Shona?"

I turned slowly, goosebumps crawling across my skin.

She was standing behind me, her red hair wild across her face. An unsettling smile twisted the corners of her mouth.

"Her name's not Shona—" Jackson started but she raised a hand to silence him.

"I can speak for myself," she said. "My name is Agnes Dowell, and I cannot begin to tell you how much of a pleasure it is to finally meet you properly."

"Dowell?" I repeated. My stomach sank.

"Yes, Tyler. You and I, we're family." She held her arms out towards me. "In fact, we're all your family. Distinguished members of the Dowell bloodline."

"I wouldn't say distinguished," Jackson sniggered under his breath.

"Have you got something to say?" Agnes snapped. In a flash, she was nose to nose with Jackson, a fire in her eyes. "Look at you, pathetic little Jackson Weir. Why are you even here? This is family business, maybe you should wait outside."

"He's my friend," I said, putting myself between them. "He stays."

She thought for a moment and backed away.

"Very well, if you say so," she said reluctantly.

"Why am I here?" I asked, cutting to the point.

"You are here because I need you," she replied. "There is a power in Lochview, a power beyond your wildest dreams, just waiting to be unlocked, and you, Tyler Buckland, *you* are the final piece of the puzzle. In all the centuries the Dowell family fought against the creatures lurking in the shadows, not once did they cross that line. Not once were they brave enough to use the monster's own dark powers against them. But I was."

Agnes paused for a moment, looking around at the others.

"They called me a witch," she said quietly. "They threatened to burn me at the stake, my own family. Do you even understand? The body is an anchor for the soul, engulfed in those flames I'd be nothing, lost without a trace. So, I ran. I surrendered myself to the depths of the loch. When my body washed up on the shore my father buried me here, a secret place away from prying eyes."

As Agnes hung her head, I almost began to feel sorry for her. There was a real pain in her voice.

"Even from beyond the grave, I never stopped. Over the years I have found others who not only share my blood but also my vision." She pointed to the others standing around the room. "I found Charles, I found James, I found Francesca and Lucille, and now we have found you. Join us, Tyler. Let us show you the power that awaits."

She reached out towards me, a soft smile on her lips. For a moment I considered taking her hand, but Jackson snapped me out of it.

"What if he says no?" he asked.

Shona's hand fell away, her smile faded almost as quickly as it had appeared.

"Why would he?" She retorted.

"Because he's not the first person you've asked." Jackson moved past me. I could see the fire growing in Agnes' eyes. "All those missing children across the years, how many stood where Tyler stands now? How many said no, only to never be seen again?"

"I would step away if I was you," Agnes warned.

"Not until you give us an answer," he challenged. "You don't scare me, Agnes Dowell. I'm already dead."

All of a sudden, Agnes snapped.

"How dare you!" she cried. Her eyes set alight with a green glow. "I will not be questioned by the likes of you!"

She placed her hand on Jackson's forehead. He screamed in pain as his body went limp, then in a piercing flash of light, he was gone. Vanished into thin air.

Agnes was breathing hard. She lent on the crypt as she tried to catch her breath.

I opened my mouth to speak but no sound came out. There were no words to be said.

"I'm sorry," she said, with a deep breath. "But I can't let anyone stand in our way."

"What did you do?" I stuttered.

"I did what I had to," she replied. "Now you have no choice but to help me."

"Why would I help you?" A mixture of fear and anger churned inside me. "He was my friend!"

"I know," she said. "And I'm the only one who can bring him back."

Her words hit me hard. I knew in that moment I was trapped. If this was a game of chess, that was checkmate. In the silence that followed, I simply stared at her, my eyes fighting hard to hold back the tears.

"Tyler, we have waited so long for this moment. You have barely even begun to scratch the surface when it comes to Lochview's secrets. There is a world out there far beyond your understanding, join us and we can discover it together." She reached out her hand. "With this power I can finally reclaim what is mine, return a true Dowell to the manor once more, and in thanks, you will earn a place at my table, a chance to take whatever your heart desires."

As she promised me the world I couldn't help thinking of the stones above my head. The innocent names carved into their faces. The victims of the girl stood before me.

"Why did you take Jackson?" I asked.

She paused and thought for a moment.

"To get to you," she said coldly. "He may have brought you into my path, but his meddling was proving dangerous. He knew too much, and you weren't ready yet. So, I had to step in. Sometimes, in the pursuit of power, you have to make sacrifices, and Jackson had served his purpose."

I felt like I was going to be sick. Jackson was a human being, more than that he was my friend and she had just squashed him like a bug that was ruining her picnic.

"Let's begin, shall we?" Agnes said, breaking the silence. "Believe me, Tyler, this will all feel much easier once it's over."

I glanced over to the empty point of the pentagram, my feet felt heavy as I dragged them forward with each step. What else could I do? She had won. It was time to accept my fate.

The body is an anchor for the soul.

The thought hit me as I took my final step.

Suddenly I knew what I had to do.

"Brothers and sisters, though separated by time we are unified in one great cause..." Agnes started, as the others began chanting.

"I'm sorry, Jackon," I muttered under my breath as I grabbed one of the flaming torches from the wall.

"Tyler, stop!" Agnes cried, but it was too late.

I drove the torch through the crack in the crypt, burying the flames underneath the broken stone.

I leant backwards, covering my face, braced for whatever came next.

But there was nothing.

Agnes lumbered towards me, her hand outstretched and her eyes glowing with menace.

I fell backwards as she reached over me. Her fingers spread like talons, ready to strike.

Then she stopped.

An explosion of green flames burst from the crypt.

"No!" she screamed. "No, please!"

She looked down at her arm as her skin began to shrivel, pulling tight against her bones. An invisible power started to drag her backwards, she stretched and clawed at the stones but it was no use, try as she might she was slowly but surely claimed by the flames.

With one final ear-piercing scream, she was gone.

They all were.

I lay alone on the cold stone floor, weak and exhausted.

I could see the moon and the stars past the top of the stairs.

And then everything faded to black.

28

I could hear the sound of flames crackling.

Opening my eyes I found myself curled up on a sofa back at the manor, Kaya sat by my feet with her nose deep in a book. As I lifted my head she turned around.

"Archie, he's awake," she called towards the open door. "Tyler, can you hear me? Are you OK?"

"What happened?" I asked. I tried to sit up but moving too much resulted in a pounding in my head.

"I could ask you the same thing," Kaya said. "We didn't like the thought of you out there on your own, so we went looking for you. You were lying unconscious in some old tomb."

I tried to think back, but every time I got close to remembering it was like my brain crashed.

Take it slow and start at the beginning.

I remembered leaving the manor. I remembered running through the woods. I remembered being on the island. I remembered the ghosts, the tomb, Jackson, Shona.

No. Not Shona, Agnes!

"Knock, knock," Archie said, arriving at the doorway. "Welcome back. How are you feeling?"

"My head hurts," I said.

"I'm not surprised." He pushed his glasses down his nose and looked at me. "We found you out cold down there. You must have taken quite the tumble."

"Like you wouldn't believe." I tried to laugh but instantly regretted it as a pain shot down my side.

"I don't want to push you..." Archie started awkwardly. "Is everything OK? Do we need to–"

"It's over," I said, cutting him off.

He went to speak but then looked at me and stopped. The last thing I wanted to do was talk about what had happened down there. In reality, I was still trying to process it myself. I think on some unspoken level Archie understood that.

"Good," he said with a nod.

I nodded back and a silence fell between us.

That was until Kaya interrupted.

"OK but as soon as you are feeling better, I want to know exactly what happened down there."

We all looked at each other and laughed. It felt good sitting there with just the two of them. It felt safe.

I just wished Jackson could have been there to enjoy it too.

"I'm going to put some tea on, would either of you like to join me?" Archie asked, breaking me away from my thoughts.

"No, thank you," Kaya replied, still giggling.

"I should probably head home," I said. I could see it was dark outside, but I had no idea how late it was. "What time is it?"

Archie glanced down at his watch.

"Oh, it is getting on," he said, raising his eyebrows. "It's nearly midnight."

"Midnight?" I swung my feet around and went to get up. "My parents are going to kill me."

No sooner had I stood up than I felt my head go light, and little stars started to appear.

"Careful!" Archie cried as he reached out to grab my arm. "Let's take it slowly, shall we?"

"That's probably a good idea," I agreed.

"OK then. I'm going to grab my car keys, and then I can drop off Kaya once we have you home." Archie sat me back down and then walked out into the hallway.

As he left, Kaya turned to me.

"I know I said thank you before, but I just wanted to say it again. You know, for saving me. Well, I guess for saving everyone now," she smiled. "You're turning into a bit of a hero."

"Thanks, but I wouldn't say I'm a hero," I replied. A hero would have found a way to save Jackson.

"No, maybe you're right." She nodded. "But, maybe with a little bit of practice, you'll get there one day."

She smiled warmly.

"Maybe." I smiled back.

"I do need you to promise me one thing, though," she said. Her grin fading.

"OK," I said, nervously.

"The next time you go running out to fight some ghost or monster. You're taking me with you."

"Deal," I chuckled.

Archie came back in with the keys, and we all headed out.

Whilst Kaya waited in the car Archie walked me to my front door. Before I could reach for the handle, he stopped me.

"Tyler, I don't know what happened on that island tonight. Nor is it any of my business. But, just in case you wanted to tell someone, I got you this." He reached into his coat a pulled out a small brown paper package. "Hopefully it helps."

"Thank you," I said, turning it over in my hands. "What is it?"

"Just a little something." He smiled. "Don't worry about it tonight. Find yourself a nice quiet spot tomorrow and open it then."

I gave a small nod and smiled back at him.

Then the front door swung open, ruining the moment.

"Where have you been?" My sister demanded.

"I was up at the manor..." I replied sheepishly.

"Don't lie to me. You are in so much trouble, you can't even imagine." Her face twisted into an evil grin. "I told you I was watching, I told you and you still did it anyway."

"Did what?" I asked, confused.

"I saw you running into the woods." She announced victoriously. "Mum and Dad are going to kill you, you're going to be grounded for a month, at least."

My mouth went dry, I tried to come up with an excuse, but my mind had nothing.

"Sorry, can I interrupt for a moment?" Archie asked, leaning between the two of us. "I'm afraid you must be mistaken, young lady. You see Tyler has been with me all evening."

It was Emily's turn to be lost for words. Her mouth dropped as she tried to argue but she couldn't. Who were Mum and Dad going to believe? Archie or her?

"No, but I saw him." She replied.

"I'm afraid that may be something you need to get used to living here in Lochview," Archie said. "Sometimes we see things that cannot be explained."

He smiled at me with a wink and made his way back to the car, bidding us goodnight as went.

I pushed past my sister into the kitchen.

"I know it was you," she growled under her breath.

I shrugged my shoulders.

"That's impossible. I was with Archie."

29

The next morning I did exactly as Archie had said. Mum and Dad were up bright and early to start decorating the café, so I seized my chance to get out into the open air. With my bag thrown over my shoulder and the brown paper package in my hand, I headed down to the loch, down to the spot where, only a few days ago, I had spent an entire afternoon with Jackson.

Standing on the shore I looked out over the water, after everything that had happened it felt different now. It was bright and peaceful, like a dark cloud had been lifted.

I took a seat on the fallen tree and, for just a moment, watched as the small waves lapped at the stones on the beach.

Loch Dowell stretched for miles off into the distance, cutting through mountains and forests, and for the first time it struck me just how big it was. Just how many secrets could be hidden in its depths.

Agnes had told me that there were things here beyond my wildest imagination, and I believed her. I had ended the reign of the Lady of the Loch, but I had a feeling that was barely scratching the surface of what Lochview had in store.

The thought scared me a little, but it excited me more.

I looked down at the package Archie had given me. I turned it over and slowly peeled off the tape.

Pulling back the paper revealed a black leather book. On the front, etched in gold, was the Dowell family crest. That familiar shield emblazoned with a lion standing proudly. Opening to the first page I found five simple words.

The Lady of the Loch.

But the rest of the book was empty. Except, that was, for a piece of card tucked away inside the back cover. A small note from Archie.

The first page is written, the rest is up to you.

I smiled down at the blank pages in front of me, waiting patiently for my story. I imagined the book sat in the library up at the manor. My tale becoming another part of the history of Lochview.

It was kind of cool. The thought of being a part of something like that.

I reached into my bag, searching for a pen, but as I did a dark shadow flew overhead.

Gazing up I saw the silhouette of a peregrine falcon, gliding through the clear blue sky. It felt like a reminder.

I might not have been able to save Jackson, but I could remember him, and with this book, I could make sure he was remembered for years to come. Taking him was the biggest mistake Agnes ever made because the truth is, if it wasn't for him, I'd have never been able to stop her.

With a warm feeling inside, I looked down at the first blank page. Yet, despite the pen in my hand I just sat and stared at the empty paper.

I didn't know where to start.

The last few days felt like a blur, so much had happened that I wasn't sure I even knew how to put it into words.

So, I took a deep breath.

I put pen to paper.

And I started at the very beginning.

It was moving day.

Tyler Buckland returns in
The Trickster and the Thief

Ready For More?

Scan below to keep up to date
with all things Lochview!